MW00473210

Anubis

Anubis

A Desert novel

Ibrahim al-Koni

Translated by
William M. Hutchins

The American University in Cairo Press
Cairo   New York

English translation copyright © 2005, 2014 by
The American University in Cairo Press
113 Sharia Kasr el Aini, Cairo, Egypt
420 Fifth Avenue, New York 10018
www.aucpress.com

First published in Arabic in 2002 as *Anubis*
Copyright © 2002 by Ibrahim al-Koni
Protected under the Berne Convention

All rights reserved. No part of this publication may be reproduced, stored in
a retrieval system, or transmitted in any form or by any means, electronic,
mechanical, photocopying, recording, or otherwise, without the prior written
permission of the publisher.

Exclusive distribution outside Egypt and North America by I.B.Tauris & Co
Ltd., 6 Salem Road, London, W2 4BU

Dar el Kutub No. 14517/13
ISBN 978 977 416 636 5

Al-Koni, Ibrahim
        Anubis: A desert novel / Ibrahim Al-Koni; translated by William
    M. Hutchins—Cairo The American University in Cairo Press, 2014
        p.   cm
        ISBN: 978 977 416 636 5
        Arabic Fiction
        I. Hutchins, William M. (tr)
        892.73

1 2 3 4 5   18 17 16 15 14

Designed by AWH Hughes
Printed in Egypt

Part Three: Grave Talk   **97**

   1 *Early Morning*
   2 *Midday*
   3 *Afternoon*
   4 *Sunset*
   5 *Evening*
   6 *The Slip*
   7 *False Dawn*
   8 *Morning*

Part Four: Aphorisms of Anubis   **169**
Glossary of Tuareg Terms   **183**

Translator's Note

IBRAHIM AL-KONI WAS BORN in Libya in 1948. A Tuareg who writes in Arabic, he spent his childhood in the desert and learned to read and write Arabic when he was twelve. After working for the Libyan newspapers *Fazzan* and *al-Thawra*, he studied comparative literature at the Gorky Institute in Moscow, before working in Moscow as a journalist. In Warsaw he edited a Polish-language periodical *al-Sadaqa*, which published translations of short stories from Arabic, including some of his own.[1] Since 1993 he has lived in Switzerland. His novel *The Bleeding of the Stone* was published in the United States in 2002, at least six of his titles have appeared in French, and at least eight are available in German translation. Representative works by al-Koni are available in thirty-five languages, including Japanese. His published works in Arabic, which are primarily literary, already number into the fifties, with publication dates ranging from 1974, for a collection of short stories, to the present.

Writing in *Le Nouvel Observateur*, Juan Goytisolo referred to Ibrahim al-Koni as a great artist whose works deserve to be known by European readers and remarked on the inexorable way his characters move from bad to worse,[2] since the final disaster comes as a surprise that seems in retrospect inevitable. Jean-Pierre Péroncel-Hugoz, in a review in *Le Monde*, greeted the release in French translation of *L'Oasis Cachée* ("The Lost

Oasis") with praise for the universal significance of a work truly presaging the emergence of Arabic literature from its "Oriental rut."[3]

Awarded a Libyan state prize for literature and art in 1996, al-Koni has received prizes in Switzerland for two of his books, including the literary prize of the Canton of Bern. He was awarded a prize from the Franco-Arab Friendship Committee in 2002 for *L'Oasis Cachée*.

The Tuareg are pastoral nomads who speak Tamasheq, a Berber language written in an ancient alphabet and script called Tifinagh.[4] They are distributed through desert and Sahel regions of parts of Libya, Algeria, Mali, Niger, and Nigeria. An estimate from 1996 put their numbers at one million and a half.[5] Their affiliation with Islam has been enriched by a vibrant mythology and folklore. The Tamasheq language is also related to ancient Egyptian. The goddess Tanit, revered in ancient Carthage, was once worshiped by the Tuareg along with the male sun god Ragh. Traditional Tuareg society has been marked by caste divisions between nobles, vassals, blacksmiths, and slaves. Tuareg men are famous for wearing veils. Women do not normally wear veils but have headscarves.

In Tuareg lore, Anubi is the archetype for sons of unknown fathers.[6] Anubi's search for his father is legendary among the Tuareg, as is his marriage to Tin Hinan, the founding matriarch of the Tuareg people.[7] The oasis featured in the second part of the novel is Targa, known to the Tuareg people as the legendary lost oasis that provides the consonants that give the Tuareg people their name: Tuareg.[8] The lost law of the Tuareg people is a Torah-like body of maxims and decrees. It has probably been more influential lost than had it survived physically.

In a book on spirit possession among the Tuareg, Susan J. Rasmussen says: "Spirits of solitude bring illnesses of the heart and soul." She explains that besides the Islamic jinn, or genies, there are other spirits in Tuareg lore: spirits "of solitude or the wild . . . who remain in isolated and deserted places." She observes that "Men's spirits cause them to become antisocial or to go out and beat people. . . ."[9] Al-Koni illustrates each of these points with his character Anubi, who arguably falls prey to these spirits.

The ancient Egyptian god Anubis, with whom Ibrahim al-Koni identifies the Tuareg ancestor Anubi, was the jackal-headed protector of the dead, who was said to be the illegitimate son of Osiris, the god of agriculture, and his sister Nephthys, the wife and sister of Seth, brother of and archrival to Osiris. Osiris was married to the goddess Isis, who was famous for her faithfulness in tracking down the pieces of his body after he was maliciously slain by Seth and for clandestinely rearing their son Horus. Seth, who was eventually defeated by Horus, is traditionally seen as a villain, but since he is also god of the desert he is of special interest to al-Koni, who has written a companion novel with Seth as lead character.[10] That Seth was also the god of thunder and lightning is of interest, since lightning plays a key role in *Anubis*.

Translating al-Koni poses several challenges to the translator. There are issues of technical vocabulary and information concerning flora and fauna; for example, would there normally be more than one adult male gazelle in a group as portrayed in a scene? The answer is that Dama gazelles congregate in large groups that include more than one male—during the rainy season, according to one source, during the dry season according to another. Are there both hares and rabbits in the Sahara? It would seem that there are only hares. Al-Koni employs technical vocabulary of another sort: words he uses in his own special way with his own meanings, and there is a template of Tuareg culture to which the translation must remain true. For example, in the first chapter, the narrator refers to his mother as *al-rabba* ("the lady"), but in a way that implies that she is a priestess, or in the manner a Christian might refer to the Virgin Mary as "Our Lady of Lourdes." Furthermore, an adjective used to describe the horizon later turns up describing the nipple on a breast. Maxims embedded in the story should read as though the character actually spoke them and yet retain the solemnity of a sacred revelation. In the final chapter of Part III, the narrator Anubi says, "We must slay our father in order to find him," a line of dialogue that also sounds like a solemn and prophetic revelation. Finally, the translator needs to remain conscious of the different layers of meaning at play in a novel, for a chase across the desert is also a metaphysical quest.

Notes

1. Ewa Machut-Mendecka, "The Visionary Art of Ibrahim al-Kawni," *Research in African Literature*, Fall 1997, vol. 28.3, p. 141 ff.

2. Juan Goytisolo, "Passion dans le desert: Un étonnant roman libyen," *Le Nouvel Observateur*, September 9, 1998; review reproduced online as of 6/12/2004 at
   http://maaber.50megs.com/tenth_issue/books_14f.htm.

3. Jean-Pierre Péroncel-Hugoz, "Al-Koni, au-delà de son islamité," *Le Monde*, 11 October 2002.

4. Johannes Nicolaisen and Ida Nicolaisen, *The Pastoral Tuareg: Ecology, Culture, and Society*, The Carlsberg Foundation's Nomad Research Project (New York & London: Thames and Hudson, 1997, and Copenhagen: Rhodos International, 1997) Vol. I, pp. 43–45.

5. Ibid., I, p. 19.

6. Ibid., II, p. 722.

7. Ibid., II, p. 722.

8. Ibid., II, p. 722.

9. Susan J. Rasmussen, *Spirit Possession and Personhood among the Kel Ewey Tuareg* (Cambridge: Cambridge University Press, 1995) pp. 47, 115, 11,129, and 12; as well Nicolaisen II, 519–20, 560–61, and 685–98.

10. Ibrahim al-Koni, *al-Bahth 'an al-makan al-da'i'* or *Aqni'a Sit al-Sab'a* ("In Search of the Lost Place") (Beirut: al-Mu'assasa al-Arabiya li-l-Dirasat wa-l-Nashr, 2003.)

Contents

Translator's Note   vii
Author's Note   xv

Part One: Cradle Talk   1
   1   *Sunrise*
   2   *Forenoon*
   3   *When the Flocks Head Home*
   4   *Late Afternoon*
   5   *Dusk*
   6   *Night*
   7   *Last Watch of the Night*
   8   *Dawn*

Part Two: Passionate Talk   49
   1   *First Light*
   2   *Midday*
   3   *Afternoon*
   4   *Evening*
   5   *Dusk*
   6   *After Midnight*
   7   *Daybreak*
   8   *Morning*

*For the spirit of the father who was a
spirit for all fathers: A.B.*

Author's Note

MY EFFORTS TO RESEARCH this legend will fill another whole book even longer than this novel, if I am ever destined to write it.

I heard bits of the legend from the mouths of matriarchs of the desert region of Tinghart during the early years of my childhood. I heard other segments from tribal patriarchs of Azjirr when I was an adolescent. What I heard from these leaders of the people heightened my curiosity for two reasons. First, the age of the legend reached back to primeval times and antedated other folk legends that appear, for example, in "Tannas and Wannas," which has entranced every poet capable of discerning the legendary aspects of daily life and the everyday experiences incorporated into legends. Second, this legend evolved over time as oral renditions transformed it and as the spirit of each age shaped it, so that the true nature of the original was shaken, the sequence of incidents disrupted, and the thread of the plot tangled. This is always the case with the oral transmission of stories claimed by several rival peoples alternately joined by alliances and then separated by conflicts.

I remember that when we settled in the oases and I began to discover the talismans of a form of writing (Arabic) that differed from the legendary symbols used in the Tifinagh alphabet, which I had learned from my mother like any other Tuareg child, a longing to ascertain the truth about Anubis quickly pervaded my heart. So I set off to search throughout my immense desert, like the treasure-hunting adventurers with whom the Sahara swarmed in those days, but with one small difference. Those adventurers relied on maps expertly drawn on skins when they tried to find their treasures, whereas the treasure I sought was an invisible wisdom rooted in my heart, while its stem flowed from the mouths of nomadic groups traversing the labyrinthine desert. I had to pursue them, to spare no effort to track them down, and then to wander wherever they went, if I wanted to gain my authentic treasure. This is what I did. I made forays in every direction by camel and crossed the desert accompanied by a few of my relatives, visiting the most far-flung tribes in Azjirr, Aïr, Adagh, and Ahaggar, so that I could question their leaders, elders, and sages.

In Timbuktu, some shaykhs showed me, hidden away in old wooden boxes, pieces of worn, crumbling leather on which faded Tifinagh symbols were inscribed. They told me this text was considered the most ancient recorded version of the legend and that it had reportedly been copied down from inscriptions—found in the caves of Tassili, in the caverns of Akukas, and on the boulders of Masak Satfat—that had been marred by rains, flooding, wind-driven sand, and the hands of vandals and mischief-makers.

In Aghades, rhapsodes and wily shepherds cautioned me about the difficulty of extracting an account of the life of our ancestor Anubi from the legends of the desert peoples, since his story has frequently been mixed with legends of epic battles and with stories about ancient heroes. Although I understood the importance of this admonition, I did not give up. I recorded everything I heard from the tongues of the rhapsodes. I accompanied sages to the caverns to decipher the symbols that had escaped destruction, comparing the versions found there with the oral tradition. I also recorded the stories in the documents that the scholars in Timbuktu translated for me from the oldest known form of the language and what I heard from the matriarchs of the tribes of Ahaggar in Tamanghasset.

I devoted an even longer period of time to piecing together the narratives, ironing out the time sequences, and shaping the individual incidents into a coherent story, rendering this once more in my mother tongue. Then I set all this aside for even longer. I did not come to grips with it again until a few years ago, when my migrations between major cities of the world (instead of between desert oases) had exhausted me. It was then that I discovered in the story of our forefather Anubi aspects of my own story (and of the story of any person who thirsts for truth). So I translated it from my mother tongue into Arabic, since I felt certain that Anubi's journey is nothing other than man's journey through this desert that people call "the world," that Anubi's tribulations in searching for the answer to his riddle are mankind's tribulations in search of our riddle's answer, and that the tribe of Anubi is, actually, the human tribe, which has yet to discover its secret truth, although we have searched for this since primeval times.

The Swiss Alps
2002

Part One
Cradle Talk

The Lord God fashioned Adam from the dust of the earth and blew the spirit of life into his nostrils so that Adam became a living being.

Genesis 2: 7

1　Sunrise

I AWOKE FROM MY SLUMBERS at sunrise and had to struggle to open my eyes. Then I watched a hesitant, golden radiance stretch across the band of the horizon to flood the naked, eternal desert strewn with ash-gray pebbles. The melancholy barrenness shocked me, but I was overjoyed to see streams of golden light pour across the exposed land and inundate an awe-inspiring world, which was mysterious despite its nudity, perhaps because it spread and stretched out endlessly, with no tree or boulder to obstruct its forlorn progress till it reached the blue sky, which was also bare and just as severe. Wishing to remain in harmony with the lower world, it seemed, the upper world had mimicked its nakedness, inscrutability, and clarity.

Had I not observed on that day the breathtaking light that hovered as importunately as a busybody between the heavenly and the earthly realms, I would have judged each a puppet of the cunning type used to create shows to beguile the young. But in their heated embrace I discerned a secret that exercised my mind for a long time before I discovered that it was an especially cryptic talisman. I found myself ever further from the secret's truth the closer I thought I was to grasping it, until I realized at last that it was at this moment when I met the mysterious puppet at sunrise, rather than at any other, that the sky and its consort the desert showed me their secret.

Perhaps that secret prompted the laugh that burst from me then. In the tent, it caused a clamor that shook me so profoundly that I expressed my alarm in a prolonged bout of weeping, even though the priestess, whom I saw standing above my head, did everything she could to restore my peace of mind. She appeared inscrutable as well, but I observed in her look a magic appropriate for a priestess. Actually it was nobler than magic, poetry, or maternal wisdom of the breast, from which I sucked my appetizing nourishment, for she was not merely a priestess. As I was to discover, she was my lady who appeased my hunger and protected me from fear. In my lady's expression I perceived a lofty look. The disk of the sun had to roll across the desert sky many times before I realized that this look is named "compassion."

Let us postpone our discussion of compassion's story temporarily, since I have not yet finished recounting the string of wonders I witnessed the day I opened my eyes to the sunrise.

When the clearly demarcated horizon split with the first effusion of the flood of light, the nakedness uniting the realms of the upper and lower world was sundered and the last remnants of the darkness cloaking the desert world dissipated. Then I passed into the spirit world to witness the miracle: to see the secret smile, the genuine smile I was destined never again to see as I saw it that day. I was destined, likewise, never to forget it. Whenever I recalled it, I always experienced that nameless tremor again. Eventually I understood that the birth of light on the desert's horizon that day was not just the birth of an awe-inspiring disk, to which the people apply the name "Ragh," but the birth of light in my heart and of a riddle in my soul. I did not perceive, until after torrential floods had overflowed the ravines, that the desert with its horizon kissed by the morning light was not another body separate from my own and that the ray of light escaping from its eternal jug was not a reality separate from mine. The sword that smote the darkness of falsehood and limited the intimate congruence between desert sky and desert land did not burst forth from some spot in the eternal unknown but from inside me. The deep delight that overwhelmed me at that moment—a delight I was not destined to savor again—was no more nor less than a profound response to my experience of this riddle, which showed me that the birth of light on the horizon was actually my own birth, that the emergence of this disk Ragh from the band suggesting the horizon was my prophecy, that the bathing of the desert's body by torrents of light was my miracle, and that the astonishing game termed "sunrise" by men's tongues was my own awakening.

What could prevent my lips from smiling once my heart had smiled? What could prevent my heart from smiling when the inner light had smiled?

Yes, this was the secret of the smile that preceded the laugh that so convulsed the consciousness of the encampment that people broke into an uproar that toppled the settlement's tent posts. Then I wept in alarm at the collapse of the settlement's dwelling, which was nothing more than a tent, and found that my lady took me into her compassionate embrace, making of her arms a cradle for me. She even crooned to me, rocking me as she hummed, soothing me, and gradually restoring calm to me once more.

The uproar in the tent, however, was greater the second time, when the supreme star rose to wend its way through space, and I found myself emitting, without meaning to, a cry that the people of the spirit world considered a prophecy: "Iyla! Iyla!"

A profound silence reigned; then clamor broke out. The shadowy figure beside my lady asked, "Did you hear that?"

The priestess, without ceasing to rock me, replied, "I heard!"

Silence reigned once more, but the shadowy figure refused to yield to it, "He spoke!"

The tent's priestess acknowledged this with a coldness that attempted to mask a happiness that could not be concealed, because it was of the same unbearable kind, "He spoke!"

Silence returned to dominate the world, but silence is fated to die at any moment, although it always wagers that a day will come when it achieves eternal victory. Silence died this time too, since the ghostly figure beside the tent post refused to remain silent. "What did he say?"

Encircling my body with her arms, my lady replied, "He spoke the prophecy!"

The apparition squatting beside the tent post remained quiet for a long time before marveling, "The prophecy?"

My compassionate lady rocked me and hugged me to her bosom. I felt such deep warmth I can compare it only to the feeling that overwhelmed me the moment the sky's heart opened to disclose the sky's secret and that of her consort the earth. Eventually my lady responded, "He spoke in the Name."

"The Name? But what name?"

I detected a note of respect in the lady's tone: "The Name that cannot be preceded or followed by falsehood."

"But is prophecy of the Name a good or a bad omen?" The lady did not reply.

She did not reply, because she had decided to take on the mission of compassion: she began to teach me the names. She called in my ear as loudly as she could, "Rau . . . Rau . . . Rau . . . Rau . . . . From today on your name is Wa." Next she struck her chest with her hand and howled into my ear, "My name is Ma." Turning toward the ghostly figure squatting beside the post, she shouted his name in my ear: "This fellow is Ba." Then she took two steps toward the entrance of the tent and carried me outside to bathe me in a flood of the light emanating from the amazing golden disk. Finally she shouted as loudly as she could, "This one is nameless, for he is master of all the names. He is the one you called Iyla. You shall call him Ragh once your speech clears and you regain an ability like mine to make the 'r' sound."

2   Forenoon

WITH THE ASSISTANCE of my Ma, I began to rehabilitate my tongue, for I had lost control of it during my journey through the unknown. I remembered obscurely that I had once mastered this astonishing organ, even though I did not know how I had lost control of it. Apparently, while I slept I had lost the tongue's secret along with the secret of my prior existence. I attempted to recall my previous day with heroic courage, but gained nothing for my heroism save a cryptic sign comparable to the prophetic one I had detected in the mien of the sky when it embraced its consort the desert as I awoke to testify to the birth of Iyla from the horizon's belly. Every time I recklessly attempted to recapture lost time, I experienced insane visions of specters, my body was racked by anxiety, and I succumbed to a splitting headache. I escaped from these dark apparitions by returning to the womb of the desert, for fear of going mad.

An ember that suddenly flared up would occasionally dispel the foyer of shadows and disperse my forgetfulness. Then the desert labyrinth would allow a view of the promise, of the homeland of the promise, and of the true nature of my lost time. I noticed, however, that this inspiration was always short-lived. Since it was a spark destined to go out, the live coal's flash would last no longer than the blink of an eye. Then regret would sear my heart, leaving me with a bitter taste. I also learned from experience that each of these rare moments of inspiration was unique. I would recall them to delight in the vision. I was forced to enter the desert again to learn part of their secret, and the ravines had to flood with many torrents before I understood that these gleams from firebrands were what the desert's priests designate as "prophecy." Prophecy remains a riddle forever, even if we discover an exegesis for it, because prophecy, this awe-inspiring emanation, is not prophecy unless it is a riddle, and a riddle ceases to be a riddle once we find an exegesis for it.

For this reason, I thought I would ignore my previous life experiences, which had cost me the use of my tongue, in order to speak of my new day, which I heard the others call "birth." (Even my lady, who trilled the word in my ear as a charm, called it "birth.") I decided to use the community's language, despite my distaste for it, since I had learned that a creature who finds himself among a group of folks does not have the right to change anything, either by creating new words to replace those in common use or by making mistakes in referring to things. People consider the invention of new names a detestable heresy and an expression of hostility against the customs established over the course of untold generations. For a man's soul to seduce him into calling things by their true names constitutes another sin. This is considered not only a deplorable display of arrogance but construed as an act of blasphemy against the august law, the lost texts of which so encouraged the privileging of the language of equivocation and concealment that most of its teachings were reduced to collections of bits and pieces, of charms and symbols that defy understanding. Thus the community continued to punish an innovator who invented new names by stoning him to death. They could think of no punishment more severe than this for the presumptuous people whose souls so seduced them into disobeying the teachings of the lost law that they called things by their true names—except exile, since they were certain that exile is an even more excruciating punishment than death. There is nothing more miserable than to be born a man only to find yourself alone and isolated in the eternal desert, unable to use the sole organ that marks you as a man rather than a rock, a tree, a lizard, or a creature spawned by the jinn; although many assert that the people of the ultimate community will excel in their use of the tongue.

I confess that this exaltation of the tongue upset me and awakened old pains associated with my inexplicable loss of control over mine. To understand what had really happened, I several times committed the error of questioning the spirit world, which may be slow to act, but whose forbearance does not last forever. Instead of solving my riddle, it requited my stubbornness with an ailment called anxiety.

The first symptom of this malady was a juvenile melancholy that overwhelmed me the moment I found myself wrapped with swaddling clothes and safeguarded by the knife blades my Ma used to protect me from the enmity of evil jinn. Next came a period when my melancholy degenerated into bitter outbursts of weeping. Anxiety intensified once it was time for me to be freed from the cradle's shackles. I abandoned myself to the seductions of the eternal desert and found myself isolated and forsaken, without power or might. So I walked in my desert alone, played in my desert alone, cared for my flocks in my desert alone, learned to comfort myself by hunting lizards alone, and sang haunting laments alone, until solitude became a companion for me, as well as a father, mother, and lord. The longer I cohabited with solitude, the deeper, richer, and more mysterious became my attachment to it. The deeper, richer, and more mysterious this attachment grew, the deeper, richer, and more mysterious became my sense of anxiety. Finally I realized that anxiety is a true lord that must inevitably take precedence over all others, since it is anxiety that leads people to lords. I ascertained as well that anyone free of anxiety is unable to take a lord in our world.

I also discovered that this type of anxiety is a labyrinth more difficult to escape than to enter. Anyone who grows accustomed to it and walks partway through it necessarily finds the hidden vessels of his heart so weakened that he will never taste happiness anywhere in his world, unless it be diluted by a dose of anxiety, which is a malady that originates from an innocent question about one's origins. As the individual falls sick, this indisposition matures into a bitter longing, which inevitably leads its victim to the refuge people call anxiety, which the lost law made a precondition for obtaining the treasure referred to as the lord.

3   When the Flocks Head Home

THE RULES GOVERNING origins seem to be no less authoritative than the law's own rules. In other words, I began to discover that I had inherited my wanderlust from a source personified by the shadow squatting by the tent post, from the figure Ma referred to as Ba the day she taught me names. I did not get a good look at this creature, just a glimpse, and so it seemed fitting for me to think of him as a shadowy apparition. Even though he had not taught me the names, as my Ma had, had not hugged me to his chest, as my loving lady had, and had not immersed me in the floods of his compassion, as the priestess of eternity had, all the same, when I opened my eyes to observe my dawning, he definitely informed me in an insistent whisper that my secret lay concealed in his wretched specter and that unless I found a way to meet him, my path would be a desert labyrinth. For that reason, apparently, I succumbed to this insane fever that began with what the community terms the "cradle" and that has haunted each step of my progress through life. I doubt I will ever recover from it, since my thirst for my Ba has not been destroyed by time, which tends to destroy everything in our world. Instead, amazing though it may sound, this thirst has gained strength with time and evolved into a concern, a longing, and a belief. I have found that it courses through my blood, like a torrent through the ravines, until it pours into the mysterious sea that, not so long ago, I named "anxiety."

It is hardly surprising, therefore, that the first question I asked my Ma, when I regained control of my tongue, was: "Where did I come from?"

My mother's answer was, "Same as everyone."

Since I was not satisfied with this response, I asked, "How does everyone come?"

She replied, "From a mother and a father."

"You're my mother," I said. "Why don't I see my father nearby?"

"Because absence is the destiny of fathers."

"Why must fathers accept absence as their fate?"

"Because fathers, like lords, are not really fathers, unless they distance themselves."

"But I saw him once," I protested. "I caught a glimpse of him as a ghostly apparition. I swear!"

She explained, "He would not have been a father unless you had seen him. Like the lord, the father must be seen at least once to demonstrate that he is a father, but he must also disappear to prove he's a father."

I was amazed. "But why must he disappear, since he can appear?"

"We are only truly convinced by what we see but only believe in what we don't see."

"Why doesn't he stay with us forever?" I asked.

"Because he comes to convey the message to us."

I asked, "What message?"

"The message that migration is the father's choice, since he wants to be as he ought to be."

"What does he want to be?"

"To be worshiped, not loved."

"Why can't he be both loved and worshiped?" I asked in astonishment.

"Because we worship what we don't see and only love what we do see."

I protested, "But, my mistress, I don't understand."

She remained silent. Dejected, she gazed at the open coun-tryside, which was flooded by the light of glorious Ragh. As she lifted her head toward the naked sky, her wrap fell from her hair, which was braided in thick, black plaits. She said, "We worship the sky but love only the desert. The sky is our father, whom we worship, because he is far away. We worship him, because we know nothing about him. On the other hand, wherever we turn, we find the desert before us. For this reason we love the desert, and we consider her our mother."

I felt desperate, and in my desperation she detected anxiety. I was astonished that she showed me no compassion then, since I had learned compassion from her. She swept her gaze across the vast areas flooded by rays from the divine, rising sun and said, as if addressing her stern prophecy to the desert wastes, "Yes, indeed, we worship fathers but love mothers."

Her prophecy about love for mothers did not astound me, but I did not understand—until I had shed blood in my quest for the missing, ghostly apparition—why concern about our fathers should change into longing or why this longing should develop into anxiety. This passion eventually exercised such a profound influence over me that I was unable to eat or sleep. Then I found no antidote save to depart.

I followed the camel trail until I reached the herdsmen in the neighboring grazing lands. I told them the truth, explaining that I had set forth in search of a father whom I had seen only as a ghostly apparition when he entered our residence as stealthily as a thief, to flee from it just as stealthily, shortly before dawn.

Since the frequency of his visits had decreased as I advanced through the stages of my quest to learn the difference between truth and error, I now doubted whether I had ever heard him speak to my mother or had observed his shadowy form squat beside the tent post. How did the herdsmen reward my tale? They scoffed at me, laughed in my face, and said that I would never taste happiness, since it is a curse to search for a father in the desert. When they noted the anxiety in my eyes, the eldest approached and led me out into the open country. There he advised me to retrace my steps if I wished to enjoy peace of mind. He explained that a father is an anonymous envoy whose mission is to bring people like me to the labyrinth that generations of men have called the desert only to double back on his tracks and disappear forever. The shepherd also said that a father resorts to tricky stratagems to discourage forgetfulness and that mine had slipped an amulet named memory into my heart, so I would discover him there each time longing overwhelmed me. On detecting my misgivings from my eyes, he bowed his head for a time.

Then, casting me a melancholy glance, he said, "Beware of searching for a father in the desert. This brings nothing but calamities." He stared at my face for a while, noting my determined and even disapproving expression, and then watched my body tremble. So he decided to yield. He spat forcefully and then said compassionately, "Fine. It's futile to attempt to dissuade a man from something that is part of his destiny. You can follow the caravan route that heads to the southern oases, if you're not afraid of thirst. You can attempt to waylay your father at the well of Wanzir, if you're not afraid of trackless wastes. You can also return home to transform your longing into a song there, if you want to save yourself." I don't sing, however, not because I lack talent, but because I've never found a tune that can cure a disease. So I set off to the west to lie in wait for my father at the neighboring well of Wanzir, following the advice of the shepherds' sage.

Hoping to reach the place shortly before sunset, I departed as the time approached for the flocks to head home. The starkness of the earth became even more depressing, severe, and gloomy, and so I turned my eyes to the sky, which was stark and severe too. In the sky's severity, however, there is always a consolation. As the lavish floods of Ragh washed across it that afternoon, the sky became clearer, bluer, and more profound. On the next leg of the journey, the trail that the caravans' camels had dug with their heavy padded hooves crossed an area of clay soil strewn with rocks grilled by the punishing, ever-lasting disk, and marked here and there by pathetic water courses, over which rain water had run in the rare rainy seasons. Gullies appeared only to end abruptly and disappear in the next stretch, since the short-lived rains that had carved them had evaporated or had been absorbed by the ever-thirsty earth. Then I would find myself lost in a labyrinth once more. The labyrinth is anything but stingy with the wayfarer; it flings decoys in his path to mislead him. The ancestral sepulchers rise in piles of black stones scorched by the fires of immolations. They do not reach very high; their rocks have been strewn about hither and thither and dispersed by the force of the rains and storms or by the passing days, since antiquity. From time to time, tombs of more recent vintage can be seen. They are larger, and their stones lighter.

The uninterrupted plain inspired a sense of desolation but also awakened an ill-defined feeling of happiness. An eternal wasteland, reproduced in every direction, was surmounted by an equally eternal sky that mimicked it by reaching out and extending in every direction and that proceeded to kiss the clearly demarcated horizon, which formed a perfect circle. Silence seized the whole land, further suggesting that a conspiracy had been laid, and I felt as insignificant as a pebble. All the same, I would not stop. The gloom that attends sunset spread through the sky, and I did not stop. Suddenly the labyrinth abandoned its arrogant ways, and the earth opened into narrow ravines with alternating patches of green and parched vegetation.

A wretched hare sprang from one of these shrubby areas, ran between my legs as he fled south, suddenly veered to the west, and then stopped. He reared up on his hind legs and turned his head to check behind him. I watched him for a while before continuing on my way but found the caravan trail also veered toward the south and passed by the spot where the miserable creature stood. I walked forward a few steps, came alongside him, and approached him, but he did not move. With his gloomy coloring, positioned there, he resembled a statue. He gazed into my eyes curiously, provocatively, challenging me.

I picked up a rock and threw it at him. He did not move. I took a step toward him and could see his eyeballs clearly, despite the dusk. His eyes were deep, large, and unfathomable, like the eyes of a human being, like the eyes of a foreign priest. A strange gleam pulsed in them, as though the rascal wished to say something. I shut my eyes to avoid seeing his eyeballs. With my eyes closed, I reached out to seize him, but he slipped free. He did not flee as he had the first time. Instead he hopped away briskly. Actually he stumbled off rather clumsily, in a way befitting heavily laden camels. He stopped beside some herbage in a nearby hollow and began sniffing the pebbles and chewing, as if nibbling on grass or perhaps ruminating. I walked toward him until I stood over him. He stared at me, but I did not detect provocation, curiosity, or challenge in his eyes this time. They seemed, instead, to betray a lack of interest. He casually sped past my feet. I leaned over to grab him, but he dodged me deftly once more and put some ground between us. The earth felt softer, and the barren land gave way to thickets of dry plants with green sprouts on the lower branches. A passing cloud had apparently dropped a shower here and brought the dead plants back to life. The rogue took his time going here and there among the herbage, greedily stuffing his mouth in the thickets. Whenever I approached, he escaped and hopped clumsily a short distance ahead, until darkness fell and I could make him out only with great difficulty. I stalked him a little further before I came to my senses and remembered that I needed to reach the well before night fell in earnest, since I had brought no water or provisions with me. I retraced my steps, but only imperfectly, since it was too dark to see my tracks clearly. So I proceeded toward the west, in the direction the trail took.

I covered quite a distance before I found the narrow track dug by the padded hooves of the caravans' camels. I kept desperately on that trail all night long, without ever reaching the well. I was overcome by exhaustion, and my throat was dry for I had sweated profusely during my trip and felt thirsty, even though the sun had set and a congenial evening breeze was stirring. I moved off the path a couple of steps and, using my hand as a pillow, slept like a dead man. I imagined I heard a commotion and was frightened repeatedly by the howling of jackals. A bevy of girls clad in black approached me. A local girl, our playful neighbor, preceded them, laughing seductively, the way she did whenever we met among the campsites or out in the open. I did not understand how the scamp had transformed herself and assumed the cursed hare's body to stand before me like an apparition of demonic height but still with the hare's challenging expression. Then the apparition acquired the features of a man, a real man, a repulsive fellow with fiery eyes and teeth the length of knife blades. I was so terrified I awoke to find that my body, which was bathed in the rays of the god of the rising sun, was releasing its last beads of sweat. On glancing around, I observed the desolate plain, which stretched away with an ever harsher aspect. All the way to the horizon, there was no hint of a well or of life. I surveyed my surroundings and discovered that the trail I had followed all night long was not the caravan route but a track that herds of migrating gazelles had made when driven by drought to seek pasture in another land. Had that ill-omened hare, exploiting the evening's gloom, succeeded in leading me astray, luring me into the labyrinth?

I remembered my Ma's tales about the misfortunes occasioned by the nation of hares, who were not always animals. They originated long ago with a female demon who disguised herself in a hare's skin when people tried to set her on fire as punishment for luring away the sons of the tribe and selling them to the jinn tribes for treasures of gold dust, a substance this invisible tribe despises. I felt even more unlucky when I remembered that this cursed female jinni had deliberately led me to the gazelle track, because gazelles, as my mother had told me, are the livestock of the people of the spirit world. The jinn like to ride them.

To the west, across the desolate plain, figures were visible along the horizon. Streams of mirages raised them into the air, distorted and dismantled them for a time, and then reconstituted them again. Hope whispered inside me that these figures might be a caravan heading east, west, north, or south, and that I ought to catch up with it before it moved too far away.

As Ragh rose higher in the cloudless sky, the mirages persisted. I decided I ought to hurry before thirst felled me. Though the shadowy images did not vanish, the distance I traversed in search of them brought me no closer. I hurried on at a faster pace and hastened forward until midday, when the desert experienced noon's conflagrations. At that time, the capricious, fluid veils began to disperse, revealing the true nature of the shadowy apparitions. On the horizon I could make out a mountain chain that interrupted the flat desert's extension to the west, blocking its endless expanse. The earth's surface changed and was interspersed with ravines along the bottoms of which were scattered retem trees and some wild plants with dried-out tops, but which underneath had desperately fought to remain green.

I restrained myself from approaching the retem trees' plumes, which I remembered cause insanity, but could not keep myself from attacking the plants. I stripped off the dry tops and swallowed their green parts. I started to chew and chew and chew. I sucked the sap, paying no attention to all the bitter tastes I swallowed from each plant. I ate for a long time. I ate not to satisfy my hunger but to quench my thirst, although eventually I felt dizzy, dropped to the ground, and began vomiting. I threw up all the different kinds of plants I had consumed, but their bitterness flowed through my body. I went into convulsions and began to shake. I remembered what people say about the desert's poisonous plants and realized for a fact that the insanity caused by thirst is a greater handicap to clear vision than the insanity that strikes us when we ingest the twigs of retem trees.

I thought I had purged my system of all these poisons, but now my body was overwhelmed by fever. I began to stagger and sought refuge, trembling, in the shade of a retem tree. I struggled with my dizziness, sweated profusely, and then felt hungry and enfeebled, as if I had not been sweating but bleeding. In my dazed condition, I fought off shadowy apparitions and sought to escape an attack from the ugly hare's fang. He stalked me, assuming at times the body of the playful lass, then of a viper, and of the despicable female demon at other moments. I do not know how long this nightmare lasted, but when I regained consciousness, I found it was late afternoon. I imagined it was the afternoon of the next day, or the third or fourth one, because my thirst had intensified, even though my fever had gone down. It was not merely thirst but a curse more wretched than thirst. I attempted to stand up, but found I could not. So I crept forward on my hands and knees across the soft earth of the ravine, brushing against various plants. Each time I caught sight of one of the green plants, I got the shakes.

As I continued crawling, the earth grew firmer with slabs of rock here and there. Next to a shrubby retem, on some rocky ground, I discovered a pile of dung. The dung was fresh, so fresh that moisture dripped from it as I crushed it between my fingers. Beside the pile of dung, on the hard surface, there gleamed an astonishing liquid that seemed a legendary treasure. Vapor hovered over it, and I feared it would all evaporate. I fell on it and began to lap it up. It tasted bitter, but I consumed all of it. As I felt it circulate through my body, my blurred vision began to clear. When I regained my sight, I noticed the gazelle, which was standing beside the retem tree, looking haughtily toward me. No, that's not right: its haughtiness was suggested, rather, by its posture. What I observed in its large, intelligent, black eyes was an inscrutable mystery. Were they really eyes, or, a strange well that spoke in that painful language, the true language: the forgotten language? I felt inspiration course through my body just as the gazelle's urine had. I found within me the ability to understand, the ability to comprehend the forgotten language, which reconciled my tongue with the gazelle's, united my destiny to the gazelle's, and created from my spirit and the gazelle's a single spirit. It was only at this moment that the coal burst into flame and that the revelation achieved a perfect form in my heart. I remembered that a tragic story from bygone generations recounted how Wannas turned into an odious creature with the head and body of a ghoul, because he had disobeyed the advice of his sister Tannas and—when overcome by thirst during his return to the campsite where he had forgotten his amulets—had drunk the urine of a gazelle. Still chewing, the gazelle's spectral figure advanced toward me. Perhaps she was chewing her cud. She drew ever closer with her haughty figure. She was gazing into the unknown, and this expression added to the profundity, seduction, and splendor of her eyes. It was a splendor we observe only in eyes that have gazed into the eye of eternity till absence becomes second nature to them. Her black eyes grew wider and turned into a brilliant, distressing, unfathomable lake. I drank as greedily from them as I had drunk the urine moments before. I began to liberate myself, not only from pain, bitterness, and weakness but from my body as well.

I threw myself into this lake, into the sea of brilliance, distress, and mystery. Instead of a sweet sense of being inundated, I felt myself become a feather, fluttering back and forth between earth and sky.

4   Late Afternoon

I AWOKE FROM my sleep, feeling shattered . . . the way a person feels when wresting himself from the jumbled confusions of a nightmare. My body seemed sunk in the ground, as if buried under a mountain, and my limbs felt like rocks. My head throbbed with unbearable pain, and my tongue was paralyzed. Although I could open my eyes, my tongue refused to budge. What was the meaning of this?

I found myself imprisoned inside a tent within a tent. Even though I was restrained, I could see outside, through the entrance, and discern the time of day. I observed that the prophecy of Ragh was a timid flow moving through the empty countryside and therefore assumed it was morning. Was it a birth? Was it my first birth or my second? If it really was a birth, it must have been my second, since a quiet voice informed me that I had been born before. Light's prophetic message, which my eyes discerned outside, was not a lie, because its root was a hidden revelation, planted so deep in my heart that I had no right to doubt it. Another revelation was unveiled in my chest, saying that I could doubt anything except my inspiration, no matter how much I wanted to, since this would mean betraying myself.

Then . . . then my heart's revelation unveiled another treasure, for I remembered a matter of sublime importance; I remembered that I had been free. How had I become a captive? I remembered that I had liberated myself from all my burdens and had shot off. I remembered that I had floated freely through space, because I had been able to rid myself of the snail's shell that harbored me. What cunning had trapped me in the snare once again? How had my liberation been effected, how had it so transformed me that I could roam freely with neither body nor tongue, and how had this liberation changed into a tribulation that constricted my breathing as if I were weighed down by a mountain?

Then I heard a voice say clearly, "This is the price of departure."

At first, I thought that this voice issued from my chest rather than my tongue, because I was certain that my tongue was paralyzed and had not stirred. This prophecy, however, was repeated with even greater clarity, and I was able, with some effort, to ascertain that it originated with a figure—crouching in a corner of the tent—who had borrowed his features from the denizens of the spirit world. A black veil enveloped his head, and an amulet chain, which was thrust into a leather pouch, protected his body. His head was crowned with a talisman, as were his shoulders. His chest was decorated with an awe-inspiring string of these talismans. His forearms were also safeguarded by two more. Had it not been for this alarming concentration of charms, I would have assumed he belonged to one of the jinn tribes that populate the desert from Tinghart to Tiniri, but concern with the forefathers' symbols buried in these districts is a matter reserved for human priests alone.

At that moment my tongue sprang to life with a facility that took me by surprise. I heard myself ask, "To which departure does my master refer?"

The question did not surprise him, I sensed, nor was he surprised by the liberation of my tongue. He proceeded to draw some designs on the ground. Then he replied, without looking my way, "A departure to search for a father."

"But . . . who are you?"

He glanced at me for the first time, and I saw in his eyes everything that should appear in the eye of a genuine priest: mystery, sorrow, prophecy, and the pain that is said to be married to every prophecy.

He replied, "You would do well to ask yourself, 'Who am I?' instead of asking me, 'Who are you?'"

I thought that the pained look in his eyes intensified then and almost turned into real suffering. I was touched by his pain but could not grasp its cause. Then I discovered he was correct: I could not say anything for certain about myself or the world, despite the precious revelation granted me that I had been born one day, had gained knowledge one day, and had been liberated one day.

I said, "You're right, master. Who might I be?"

"I almost lost the world to return you to the world."

"I don't understand."

"Don't you remember anything at all?"

"I remember that I was free!"

I caught the gleam of a smile in his eyes. He faced toward the entrance to allow his eyes to roam the vacant wasteland. He replied, "You're not mistaken about that. You truly were free. You were so free that you almost lost yourself on account of this freedom."

"Does freedom cause us to lose ourselves, master?"

"Freedom, my son, is about living, not about dying."

"But I was happy."

"Happy like a living person or a dead one?"

"Enshrined in my memory is the treasured saying of a wise man who claimed that in happiness life becomes equivalent to death."

"Watch out! True heroism is to live, not to die."

"Are you saying that heroism is living, not dying?"

"Absolutely."

"I like that, but is it possible for us to find a place for freedom in this heroism?"

"Where did you get your ability to debate? Unless he's well along in years, it's inappropriate for a man to pelt a priest with questions."

"The child isn't the author of his questions, master. The author of his questions is the freedom dormant in the child's breast."

"This is a malady. It's a curse. Watch out!"

"Yes, of course, master. Freedom is always a disease, always a curse, but—like prophecy—it's a curse we worship."

"For boys to utter prophecy is a sign of misfortune, even if their prophecy is genuine."

"Am I a boy?"

"Your tongue has actually made me wonder whether you are."

Silence reigned. Outside, the light's color faded. So I asked, "Is it dawn or dusk?"

"Late afternoon."

"I've been feeling I'm experiencing my birth."

"Yes, that's right. You are experiencing your birth. There's no doubt about that."

"Is it my second birth?"

"Yes, indeed. You have every right to feel sure of that."

"Is the second birth paradise?"

"We cannot live once without hoping we'll be born a second time."

I repeated after him: "'We cannot live once without hoping we'll be born a second time' . . . but, master, you speak of the price we must pay for departing to search for our fathers."

"The price of searching for fathers is metamorphosis."

"Metamorphosis?"

"Yes, indeed. I had to wage a lethal combat with the most wicked jinn before I could liberate you from the evil of metamorphoses."

"Of what metamorphoses are you speaking, master?"

"Some shepherds were peacefully pasturing their flocks in Retem Ravine when they were taken by surprise by a despicable specter that terrified their animals."

"A despicable specter?"

"It was an ugly, composite creature, half-man, half-beast."

"Was it a jinni?"

Ignoring my question, he continued his tale. "He was creeping on all fours, competing for grass with the livestock. Around his neck hung some talismans. Wretch, did you drink gazelle urine?"

"Did you say 'gazelle urine'? I think I saw something wondrous in the gazelle's eye. I drank the urine and then saw the wondrous thing. Now I remember. The despicable hare crossed my path and led me off the trail. My thirst robbed me of my reason and I drank. I admit I drank gazelle urine. Had it not been for the gazelle's urine, I would not have been liberated. Had it not been for the gazelle's urine, I would not have been saved. Had it not been for the gazelle's urine, I would not have witnessed my second birth."

"You achieved your second birth, but your departure cost you your mother."

"What?"

"You will never see her again, from this day on."

I remembered again. I remembered that I had burst forth from the womb of my Ma one day. I remembered that she had taught me the names one day. I remembered that she had forbidden my search for my father, explaining that the homeland of fathers is the sky, not the desert. I remembered. I remembered.

"You set forth to find your father and thus lost both your mother and father."

"From my mother I came. By my mother I lived, and to the embrace of my mother I will return. How can I believe that I could ever lose my mother?"

"From today onwards, you will never see her again."

"I shall never believe that. But . . . what happened?"

"She only forbade you to search for your father because she was afraid of being separated from you. When she was told that you had fled to search for your father, she realized that she had lost you for good. When she went with the other women to draw water from the well, she surprised them and threw herself down its shaft."

"No!"

"You killed her."

"No!"

"You're not just any kind of killer; you're a matricide."

At that moment I liberated myself. I liberated my body this time. The oppressive weight on my chest was lifted. I sprang up like someone springing free of a nightmare.

Yes, yes, it had to be another nightmare. The nightmare had continued, and the priest crouching opposite me was just the spectral figure of one of the jinn at whom I should throw a rock or a handful of pebbles. I reached to fill my hand with pebbles, which I threw at the figure's face, but he did not disappear or dissolve the way an apparition would have. I recited a charm so ancient I did not know the meaning of the words, but he did not budge. I crept toward him until I could almost touch his intimidating turban with my head. I stared into his eyes for a long time and then asked, "Why don't you tell me how you liberated me from the metamorphoses?"

5   Dusk

As dusk descended, she chased me between the tents and pursued me out into the nearby open areas. She positioned her index finger in her mouth, just as she had so often done while a babe in the cradle. She crept after me as obstinately as a fly, just as she had done when she was still a toddler. For the twentieth time she said, "If you accompany me to Retem Ravine, I'll tell you a secret."

"You're lying!"

"You won't regret it."

"I know this trick."

"You won't regret it."

She spoke while continuing to suck on her finger. Seduction flashed in her eyes. She walked seductively and bore herself seductively. O Lord Ragh, how quickly the daughters of the desert mature! They are like desert plants that send up spiky stalks the day after it rains. Every part of our neighbor-girl had ripened and filled out: cheeks, breasts, and hips. When we were playing around the campsite, the naughty girl had grown accustomed to putting an index finger in her mouth while slipping her other hand stealthily between my legs. She would fool around there while she laughed and continued to suck on her finger. One time, I asked her straight out what was the secret of this tail boys have. She said that boys don't play with dolls because they have a tail, whereas girls want a doll, since they do not have a tail. Then, laughing shamelessly, she placed her hand between my thighs and began to press what lay there. One day when I accompanied her to the pasture, she tried to pull my clothes off. I resisted her, but she calmly tore my shirt in two and dragged me under a bushy retem tree to be alone with me there. This evening also I yielded and accompanied her to nearby Retem Ravine.

When we were alone, I asked her what the secret was. Placing her index finger in her mouth and then withdrawing it, she said, "I wanted to tell you the secret about your mother."

I replied with idiotic naiveté, "The priest told me I'd killed her."

"Never believe a priest."

"How can we doubt a priest who's the author of a prophecy?"

She entertained herself by sucking on the invisible nectar of her slender finger. Her large black eyes, which resembled a gazelle's, gazed into mine. Within her eyes there was a profound, secret treasure. She dropped her eyelids to veil the treasure. Then she withdrew her finger to say, "It was the priest who killed your mother."

I did not believe her. I suddenly felt weak. My powers flagged. I stammered, "You're lying!"

In her eyes, however, I saw what I did not want to see. I saw something the tongue could never convey. I saw the truth. I asked, "But why did the priest kill my mother?"

Sucking on her finger, she stuttered, "It was your mother who wished it."

"What?"

"To pay for your return to the world."

"What are you saying?"

"When you set out to search for your father, the men of the tribe set out to search for you. She vowed to sacrifice a she-camel to the goddess Tanit if they found you alive. When they gave you up for lost, she vowed to give her entire herd to the goddess. When you entered the pasture lands with the body of a gazelle and the head of a man, as the news spread through the tribe, she offered her neck to the priest if he would return you to the world."

"I don't believe that."

"He slaughtered her like a ewe on the tomb of the ancestors."

"Shut up."

"It's said this wily strategist sought her life as the price of your deliverance from the reign of metamorphoses."

"I asked him to tell me about my release. He said he freed me with the ancients' charms, with those only the shrewdest magicians know."

"They say that when she lay down to be slaughtered, she declared: 'It's not important whether I die. What's important is for him to live. I didn't come into the world to stay here. I came into the world so he could be.'"

We fell silent. Dusk changed into nightfall, indeed into the dark of night, but my eye could still see the treasure and the invisible universe in her eyes, just as I had seen it in the eyes of the gazelle that day.

She said, "That's not all." She closed her eyes. Her finger continued to poke around in her mouth but did not prevent her from saying, "Your father!"

She fell silent, and I could not bear it. I asked, "What do you want to say about my father?"

She replied coldly, "He followed you home after you departed."

"That's a lie."

"I know no one will ever tell you the truth. My grandmother says that we have to learn to read people's eyes, if we want to know anything."

"Why did the priest conceal the truth from me?"

"Because the priest is a member of the tribe, and the tribe does not want us to trail after our fathers, because that's a violation of the teachings of the ancient law."

"The lost law?"

"The law that everyone refers to as lost, even though its presence among us is more powerful than that of breathing."

"Who taught you this?"

"I know this because I've learned to listen. Learn to listen if you want to know things."

"I think I've also heard that the law is hostile toward fathers and anyone wishing to affiliate himself with the race of fathers."

"In the customary practice of the law, fathers have no legal standing."

"But what's the secret behind the law's hostility toward fathers?"

"For us to learn the true reason for this hostility, we must live a long time and listen a long time."

I was trembling. My body had begun to burn with emotion, fever, and misery. I asked, "But why didn't he wait for me?"

"He didn't leave until he had given up all hope."

"How did the law-abiding folk treat his arrival?"

"They thought it ill-omened."

"Ill-omened?"

"The truth is that their prophecy was soon fulfilled, because a curse fell on your dwelling the moment he left."

"What curse?"

"Is there a curse more dreadful than for the tent post to collapse and for the home to be destroyed? Is there a fouler curse than for the mistress of the home to fall? Is there any curse more evil than for the family's son to be transformed into a creature with a monster's body?"

Silence sank deep roots, and the dark of night did as well. Her distant eyes were now veiled from me, and my mind soared far away. I obstinately focused on the foyers of my first birth. I scrutinized them but gained nothing more from this trip than a vision. I gained nothing beyond that figure who had appeared to me one day, squatting beside the tent post and conversing with my mother about the riddle, back when I spoke the prophecy.

Without meaning to, I said, "I saw him one day. I saw my father once. How can I see him again?"

I heard her voice in the dark but did not see her eyes. I could not see the truth. It seemed to me I was hearing the voice of the priestess: "We only see our fathers once. A father must show us his face once, so we can lose him for good thereafter."

"I saw him like an apparition beside the tent post. He seemed to be one of the prophets."

"All fathers are prophets."

"Since then, he's remained hidden."

"Our fathers vanish, because they are prophets."

I implored the priestess of the darkness, without realizing what I was saying: "I want to see him. How can I see him? Can't the priest summon him for me?"

In the darkness, prophecy issued from the tongue of the priestess, "The priest can summon your father's shadow, but he will never be able to produce your father for you."

I was convulsed by anxiety. I trembled and fell backwards. Overhead I saw the stars.

6   Night

THOSE VIPERS KNOWN as women bit me early in life: an émigrée
visitor to the villages bit me on the hand. The tribe, for some
reason I never knew, called her Tamnukalt, or "Princess," and
treated her with respect and pomp. She was rather haughty with
an imperious bearing, a full body, a white complexion, and a
beautiful face. Her eyes had an expression I understood only
with hindsight; as that fang the tribe's sages call "lust." As I later
realized, she was able to infect me with it, because I did not
know its name. She moved from tent to tent with the grandeur
befitting a woman of her wealth, beauty, and mystery. She would
visit with the women, who treated her to banquets of meat and
to singing parties, which would occasionally last until dawn.
Several times I accompanied my mother to these parties, where
I played with friendly girls, who liked to take me off into the
corners of the tents. There I would hide with them and fall
asleep before the evening's entertainment began. My Ma would
search for me to no avail and, when she despaired of finding me,
return home alone. I would rejoin her only the next morning.

At one of these parties, the émigrée pinched me secretly on
my buttocks. The first time, I doubted whether she had actually done it, but the act was repeated several times. I was
astonished and then repulsed, but she leaned over my face
until her braids buried it. As the scent of her body assailed my

nostrils, I began to feel dizzy. I closed my eyes and found that she was putting a handful of dates on my lap. Then she brought her face so close to me that I felt her breath caressing my neck. Her lips touched the flesh of my right ear as she whispered in a sibilant voice, "If you visit me, I'll give you a lot more. If you visit me, I'll fill your arms with fresh dates dripping with honey."

That night I did not find dry dates in my lap; I found truly fresh dates. I found the most delicious fresh dates of the oases, and honey actually oozed from them, as if a generous hand had plucked them from the palm trees of distant oases and fled with them to the desert with the speed of the jinn. The fruit's delightfulness did not rest in its sweet juiciness, its tremulous mass, or its succulence, but in its taste, which I would never forget. It was a mythic taste that shook and provoked me, awakening in me forgotten moments I had not experienced in this lifetime. The taste made me sense that this birth was not my first, that I had been born a thousand years, indeed a million years, before. The suppressed memory awakened by the wondrous taste of that amazing fruit did not hail just from ancient times but harked back to ages that could not be reckoned in years and for which the concept of time itself was meaningless, to that secret entity wise men call "eternity." Could it be what these sages term "immortality"? Was the taste concealed in the fruit a magic potion created as an antidote to the fearful disease people term "forgetfulness"? Against this malady even the elixirs of the magicians have been powerless.

Does this not imply that I am a creature without end or beginning, enjoying in this respect the same status as the desert, so that my death is merely a disappearance, an inevitable consequence of being asleep, and my life is simply an appearance, an inevitable consequence of being awake?

For several days I wandered about dazed, but I could not bear to wait long. I determined that I would vanquish forgetfulness and recapture that lost life, my true life, no matter what the cost.

I went to her tent, where I found her bowing in the direction of the forenoon's Ragh to plait her luxuriant hair into slender braids. She intimated with a glance of her eye that I should approach, and I crept a few inches closer. The perfume of her body assailed my nostrils. I staggered and shut my eyes to ward off dizziness, but she stretched out her hand and seized me. With a bold palm she grasped me and pulled me into her arms. No, that was not it; I did not find myself in her arms but snuggled against her full bosom. I was inside her flowing gown, in a vale between two astounding breasts crowned with prominent nipples. My body fell atop a taut ivory expanse. I became lost in this labyrinth of ivory and slid ever farther down. I clung to the only outcropping my hand could reach and grabbed hold of her breasts, but they escaped from my hand, because they were larger than my palm. So I struggled desperately and grabbed the jaunty, protruding nipples at the tips of her breasts.

Then I heard her say in the same hoarse, sibilant voice, "The women say you like to fool around. The women say you've taught their daughters several games. Even your mother wants you to be playful, because she thinks a playful boy is a successful one. Now you can play. Hee, hee, hee." She chortled for a long time, until the chortling turned into a deep moan.

While struggling to keep from slipping ever lower, I remembered her promise and shouted to remind her what she owed me. "Dates! You promised to give me dates."

She crooned, "Is any date in the desert tastier than the one you grasp, rascal?"

The jaunty nipple escaped from my fingers, which had become slippery because of some liquid, either sweat from my hand or moisture oozing from the teat. So I skidded further down the soft, ivory-colored body. I found myself in another valley at the center of which lay a thicket of dense undergrowth. As I grasped this undergrowth, my nostrils were met by a fragrance I could taste with my tongue. It was the secret taste that disperses forgetfulness and lights the path to immortality.

I began to visit her tent every day to savor that taste until the day of separation dawned. I awoke one morning to discover that her tent had been struck and that the mistress of the taste had departed. I could not believe it, perhaps because I had never imagined I could lose this taste and fall prisoner to forgetfulness again.

Forgetfulness felt like a mountain crushing my chest, and I resolved to liberate myself. I asked which way she had headed and set off in pursuit. I raced after her like a madman but found only mirages waiting at the horizons. I became exhausted and dehydrated, while the sun-baked earth scorched my bare feet. I fell to the ground and began to creep on all fours. As I crept forward, the path skinned my knees and hands, and I began to bleed. Finally unable to proceed any further, I experienced bitterness, not the taste of the lost fruit. My only consolation lay in weeping. I wept and wept, until night fell and sleep overtook me.

7   Last Watch of the Night

I SET OUT TO SEARCH for the priest, but he had disappeared from the settlement. I consulted the nobles, but they all agreed that they knew nothing of his whereabouts. I asked the matriarchs, and one of them commented that priests are a race comparable to the jinn's offspring, who disappear whenever we search for them and reappear only when we do not expect them.

I went to the grisly tomb whose stones the priest had soaked with my mother's blood, according to the neighbor-girl's account, but did not find him there either. I traveled to the pastures and questioned the camel herders, who told me he had branded his camel with the sign of the goddess Tanit to protect her from thieves and since then had allowed her to roam untended in the desert of Tinghart for several years. I finally lost all hope of finding him and decided to bury my anxiety in forgetfulness. Since this world was the ablest assistant I had found, I headed for Targa to search for the camel my mother had given me just before that ill-omened day of separation. I had entrusted her to a fellow tribesman who said he was related to me in some way. So I headed out to the open country nearby to watch for caravans heading south.

Using my wrist for a pillow, I stretched out under an acacia tree to spend my first night. I was just drifting off to sleep, as dreams hovered around me, when the priest's figure appeared,

standing above my head. At first I imagined he was a fragment
that had split off from a dream. Then I was able to recognize
him by the light of the stars, even though he was partially concealed by his garments, which were of a gloomy color. He stood
by my head for what felt like a lifetime before he observed coldly, "I was told you've been looking for me."

When I did not reply, he dropped down on his haunches, facing me. I stared at his face in order to read the prophecy in his
eyes, to read the certainty in them, but the cloak of darkness
concealed their silent expression. So I said, "I thought priests
were people like anyone else, not specters."

Without any hesitation, as if he had been expecting this
remark, he answered, "Where would priests obtain their prophecies if they couldn't change into specters?"

I stared at him again. I thought I detected a glint of covert
disdain flash through his eyes. The sight provoked me, but I
swallowed the anger I felt like a lump in my throat and said,
"Priests have a right to turn into specters or jinn, but they have
no right to turn into killers."

"Killers?"

"You killed my mother."

I said this coldly, even though my whole body was trembling
and shaking. He continued to stare at me calmly. The disdain
visible in his eyes seemed stronger. With the same detestable
coldness he said, "Of course! Priests also kill. They only kill,
however, in order to bring someone back to life."

My body's trembling increased as I began to develop a fever.
I saw my mother dandling me. I saw her teaching me the names
of things. I saw her teaching me the prophecy. I saw her bringing me outside so I could bathe in the light of Ragh and grasping me back to cherish me in her embrace. I began to choke. I
tried to speak, but my tongue, which was all twisted up in my

mouth, failed me. So he spoke, instead of me. He spoke to complete his victory. Yes, indeed, victory always belongs to the side that speaks. Victory always falls to the side that can make the best use of the tongue. Truth is also the tongue's sweetheart. He who fails to use his tongue is left falsehood's side. So, blessings on anyone who makes excellent use of the tongue and woe to anyone who fails to employ it successfully.

The cunning strategist spoke coldly because he perceived that his coldness provoked me and that coldness could slay me, "How could I have brought you back to life without killing her?"

"Rubbish!"

It cost me a heroic effort to spit out this word, even though I knew how silly it sounded. I was certain "rubbish" was something I had uttered and not something he had said. It seems the wily strategist sensed my impotence, for he brazenly demonstrated his mastery over the tongue. "Don't you know that it was her death that restored you to life? Don't you know that the birth of children presupposes the destruction of their mothers?"

I heard this statement but did not understand its import. I did not understand, because I suddenly woke up, just as I once woke up to find myself imprisoned by my mother's embrace. I had stammered then, because I had been deprived of the use of my tongue. So, speaking for me, my mother had told the story, just as the priest was now speaking for me. The wily schemer seized the opportunity to monopolize the conversation. He talked and talked and talked, but I did not understand. Perhaps I did not understand because I did not listen. I did not listen because I was feverishly wrestling a knife from the sleeve of my robe. The fates had it that my dread knife should sink into his throat just when he had finished declaring: "This is the law of sacrifice!" So he became the sacrifice, because the weapon's blade plunged deep into his throat. The plentiful, warm, viscous blood gushed out and stained my fingers, my wrist, and even my face, flowing down to soak the desert's earth, which has been thirsty for millions of years. I had to wait a very long time to witness that haughty creature fall upon my lap: a wasted body, empty, and as light as a pile of feathers.

8   Dawn

WE MET AT THE CURVE of the ravine as she headed toward the pasture with her flocks. When she caught sight of my bloodstained shirt, she gasped in alarm but did not release her index finger, which she sucked to mask her alarm. She was hard to understand while she chewed on her finger. "What's this? Did you slaughter a kid or a billygoat?"

"Yes, indeed; I've slaughtered a billygoat. Yesterday I slaughtered a black goat."

She stared at me skeptically before continuing: "Was it a sacrifice?"

"Yes, indeed, a sacrifice."

I gazed at her black eyes, which were as deep as the gazelle's, before adding, "I slaughtered the goat as a sacrifice for my mother's spirit."

Her eyes gleamed with the sparkle we see only in gazelles' eyes. This sparkle is not to be understood, investigated, or resisted. I turned my face away and allowed my gaze to soar across the open lands in search of some inspiration to help me express my secret, "Didn't you say he slaughtered her on the tomb the way you'd slaughter a ewe?"

She stopped chewing on her finger. The color of kohl spread through her eyes, and blackness dominated them so entirely that they became even deeper, more beautiful, and more enigmatic. I got the shakes and felt feverish again.

I saw him fall to his haunches, balancing himself on the tips of his fingers opposite me, bleeding, bleeding, bleeding. Not a single moan of suffering or groan of pain escaped him when the knife settled in his throat. In fact, he stayed erect so long I was convinced he was a demonic child of the jinn. He fell in my lap, however, just when I had decided to flee. He fell into my lap like a pile of chaff or feathers. He fell into my lap as if wishing to seek refuge with me. He fell into my lap, because the slain person must seek refuge with his killer. He fell into my lap because it is decreed that slain men take refuge with their slayers.

I gazed into her eyes. I gazed until I disappeared into their depths. I pulled the knife from my sleeve and flourished it in the air as if combating an invisible enemy. In a stranger's voice I croaked, "I stabbed him like this. I stabbed him in the throat. Like this! And this! Ha, ha, ha . . . ."

I swallowed my laughter and exhaled. I blew out all my breath until I began to suffocate for lack of air. I was drenched with sweat, and my eyes found nothing to focus on until they settled on the knife fouled by the victim's blood. At that moment I heard her voice and was astonished. I was astonished, because I had forgotten her. I had thought myself alone in the wilderness and so had forgotten her. She took me by the hand and sat me down beside her on a hill overlooking the ravine. She said quite distinctly: "You don't know what you've done."

Then she paraphrased her words in the same authoritative tone, "Oh, if you only knew what you've done!"

I interrupted her, with even more authority, "I did what I had to do! I never regret an act I've committed."

She bit her finger and rocked as if ready to emit a wail of mourning, "But it's an act that makes repentance for any other deed you commit superfluous."

I did not understand her and kept silent. We were both silent for a time. I tried to catch my breath, but she showed me no mercy. "You've killed your father! You've killed your dad!"

I thought she was affecting the language that elders use when they speak equivocally. I thought she was reciting a story of past generations, one that would end with a moral, aphorism, or a saying with a hidden reference, but she turned toward me and stated with a clarity that banished all doubt, "Don't you realize that you've killed your father, wretch?"

Dumbfounded, I protested, "I don't know what you mean."

"The priest was your father."

I laughed. I laughed even though I was short of breath. I said with great certainty, "If the priest was my father, then I would never have lost my father."

"You don't understand."

"Didn't you tell me once that my father came to my house the day I set off to search for him in the desert's labyrinth?"

"I did not lie."

"You also said he followed me, to bring me back."

"I did not lie."

"But he brought back my mother, not me."

"If he had not taken your mother, he would never have brought you back. If he had not taken your mother, you would not find yourself striding through the desert on two feet."

"But how can I have searched for my father throughout the world when he was within arm's reach?"

"All the things we search for in faraway places are actually within arm's reach."

Again she had begun to speak in riddles. Once more this young vixen, who had told me she had learned to speak by learning to listen, had begun to speak in the language of the priestess, with all the certainty of the priestess.

I did not listen, however, for I could not wait to ask, "But by what right did the priest become my father?"

"Priests were created to be fathers. Those men we call our fathers actually aren't."

"Then who are the priests? Who are the fathers?"

"The fathers are shadowy figures. The priests are real."

"If you want me to understand the truth about the priests, then don't speak to me in the language of the priests."

"Fathers are always a lie."

"You're lying."

"But the priest is the master of prophecy. We are the children of prophecy. All the children of the tribe are children of prophecy. All the children of the desert are children of prophecy."

"I'd have to be a priest to understand your riddles about prophecy."

"That's why we've inherited from the ancients a saying—endorsed by our lost law—that recognizes the mother as the sole parent. We offspring are as lost as the lost law, because we are kin to prophecy on our father's side and to the desert on our mother's."

"I heard my mother say something like that."

"That's why, according to the law, you're not merely a patricide but a deicide."

"Lie!"

"He who kills prophecy kills the lord."

"Lie!"

"And that's not all."

Through this medium's eyes I detected a new danger. In the eyes of this she-jinni I beheld a new prophecy. I was shaking and feverish. I was disoriented, but even so I heard correctly what she said next, "You must understand that you killed not only your own father but mine as well."

"What are you saying?"

She cast her glance far away. She raised her index finger toward the empty space as though pointing out an unknown talisman. Then she bombarded my ears with this painful prophecy, "I'm your sister!"

Although I did not believe this, I did not enquire any further, because my chest felt weighed down. I do not know how much time I spent on that hillock. I also do not know whether it was evening or daytime, sunset, or dawn. I reflected on my reality as a creature that has been abandoned, that is lost, and that will never discover his fatherland or his father. I discovered in my reality every desert son's true nature, since he must acknowledge his misery at having lost all trace of his paternal lineage. He is destined to fall under customary law, which traces kinship maternally. He has to content himself with his lot, which is identical to that of Anubi.

I decided to flee at once from the tribe, from the desert, and even from myself. Perhaps I could free myself from my destiny. I roamed through the wasteland; I might experience a rebirth in the settlements of the land known as Targa.

I did not feel any bitterness over losing my sense of time nor did I regret losing the savor of days; I remember that I stretched out one day in a solitary place enveloped in darkness and slept as I had never slept before, unaware of the advent of evening or of the morn of the following day.

Part Two
Passionate Talk

*He said to Adam: "Since you have hearkened
to the words of your wife and eaten from the
tree I warned you to shun, saying, 'Don't eat
from it,' you have brought down a curse upon
the earth. You will need to toil every day of your
life to wrest a living from it, and it will reward
your efforts with thorns and briars. You will eat
the grass of the field. By the sweat of your brow
will you have bread to eat, until you return to
the earth from which you sprang, because you
are dirt and to the dirt you return."*

Genesis 3: 17–19

1   First Light

I AWOKE AT SUNRISE and found myself alone, abandoned, and stretched out in a harsh, solitary area into which intruded stubborn spines of sand. It was blocked to the west and north by a desert punctuated by grim mountain cliffs, around the sides of which the sands twisted in relentless swirls. A discrete, early light kissed their peaks, but the tips of the sand drifts were bathed with morning's flood, and glinting gold specks flashed there.

I awoke but lay quiet for a long time, listening to a stillness that I was prepared to believe—I don't know why—eternal, devoid of any precursor, the sole beloved ever to share the desert's solitude, since it came into existence.

Surveying my surroundings, I found no food or water in sight. When I tried to stand, my body felt as heavy as if I had covered incredible distances on foot. On touching my face, I discovered that it was enveloped by a soft mask of skin that resembled a piece of silk. I ran my palm over my chest only to find it clad in soft, rich hide stamped with symbols I did not recognize. My feet were also encased in splendid shoes of costly leather decorated with talismanic charms. I did not feel hungry or thirsty.

Overcoming the heaviness of my body, I regained my feet, got my bearings, and headed east. The golden disk was concealed behind a high ridge of sand. The sandy tentacles with

overbearing tops twisted one way and the other, but the valleys between them were grim and uninviting. All the same,
I caught sight of a green tangle of plants clinging to the
earth, which was strewn with pebbles in places and sand
granules in others.

A vast mountain of sand blocked my way. At its foot, I discovered a line of luxuriant plants, massed together. These took
the form of mounds, crowned with delicate, pure white florets
that responded to the morning breezes by bobbing back and
forth in a desperate dance, as if wishing to break free from their
roots. They sighed mournfully, affording me companionship in
the lonely desolation of the timeless quiet. From the canopy of
one I seized a handful of flowers that oozed a white liquid. I sam-
pled a piece of the stalk, testing its flavor with my tongue. The
sap was gooey and had a bitter taste.

When I tried to scale the sandy mountain, I discovered its
sand was the unstable kind that shifts and rushes downward in
a flood, sweeping everything with it. I struggled for a long time
and attempted to anchor my hands in the sand, but was always
cast back, down to the foot of the mountain. Resolving to outwit it, I relinquished my attempts to climb straight up and edged
along sideways, instead, following the protruding veins that lay
along its horizontal articulations. These led me to the summit
from which I beheld broad plains interspersed with green clusters of trees at four points. Meanwhile, on four sides, sandy
ridges also enclosed the plains, which seemed set apart from the
desert's body, which extended and multiplied until it disappeared at what passed for the horizon. To the far southwest, at
the point where the intersection of the southern mountain
ranges with the western ones should have been visible, there
was a cleft, which seemed the sole escape from this mighty
fortress contrived by the desert's cunning.

I tumbled down the prodigious slope, casting myself on the unstable, rough terrain, which rolled me down, over and over. On reaching the mountain's foot, I shot off toward the groves but did not reach them, since they were farther than I had anticipated. On the way, I found evidence that creatures inhabited the land. The traces were plentiful, but my eyes discerned not a single animal. When I reached the first clump of green, I found trees there and some shrubs. These all followed the course of a bold stream that gleamed in the sunlight. Water gushed from a natural reservoir to pour into the plain in little rivulets that ran west and east, until the neighboring sandy hills consumed them.

Copious clusters of attractive fruit, which looked delicious, hung from the tops of the trees. I stretched out my hand and plucked a plump fruit the size of my finger from a generous bunch. When I touched it, I found the clear liquid leaking from it was sticky. I popped it into my mouth and started to chew. As it dissolved beneath my tongue, it was so sweet my teeth hurt. It mixed with my saliva and began to course through my body. Chewing on it lazily, I reveled in the unusual taste. I was in no hurry to swallow the morsel, not because I did not feel hungry but because of the obscure sensation the taste awakened in my heart.

I visited the other three springs as well. Around them grew date palms in congenial groupings similar to that surrounding the first spring. From these palms dangled stalks heavy with various types of dates. Beneath the trunks of these lofty palms were scattered dates, some dry and others still fresh. On the damp earth beside the springs were tracks of the animals whose traces I had found by the rivulets rich with vegetation. I could identify them, now that I had jogged my memory, as tracks left by the feet of gazelles, Barbary sheep, hares, lizards, and various types of birds. I did not recognize them merely from their tracks but from the dung pellets distributed everywhere. Flocks of birds flapped their wings as I violated the groves' sanctuary. They would soar over my head once or twice before flying off, only to land on the canopy of the nearest spring. I encountered a large herd of gazelles in a valley opposite the last spring toward the southeast. Acacia trees proliferated there, and the gazelles roamed among the trees, some grazing off plants on the ground and others craning their necks to reach the top of the acacias and pluck the green leaves. They became skittish when they saw me and joined ranks to form a single herd. This reminded me of the way goats react to the scent of jackals. They watched me with collective curiosity but did not take fright or flee. So I felt certain they had never seen a man before. I stood, admiring the beauty of their eyes, but eventually the herd bolted and dashed away.

I traversed an open area coated with gravel composed of small round, red pebbles until I reached the base of the mountain range. What I had assumed was a sandy slope was actually a genuine mountain scaled by drifting sand. The walls forming this mythic fortress had not originally been ridges of sand but rocky mountains that the sands had seized in crazed raids, submerging the rock. Only the southern barrier had succeeded in resisting their assault, even though the wind had been able to submerge it from the back, as I discovered later.

All along the cliff face there were caves, which seemed, seen from below, to be fabulous mouths. Around their entrances lay many dung pellets, but I did not know a herd of Barbary sheep sheltered there until a huge ram with thick, matted fleece stormed out of a cave and scaled the high rocks in a couple of bounds. He stood looking down on me curiously. When I explored the cave, I discovered that its walls were decorated with numerous colossal figures. These were strangely contrived creatures: legendary animals and women. Men pursued Barbary sheep, or—brandishing spears—danced in groups. There were other creatures concocted by matching men's bodies with animal heads crowned with horns or with birds' heads. I stood for a long time examining these unnatural, composite creatures.

These designs coated the cavern from the top of the ceiling to the foot of the sides and extended the length of the rock walls, which were cloaked in darkness they ran so deep inside.

Outside I craned my neck, examining the cliff face, until noon and time for the midday heat. Then I decided to take a break and sought refuge in the nearest cave, where, from the entrance, I found myself facing a shadowy figure I could not make out clearly, since it was so dark; as I leaned against a wall of the cavern to catch my breath, I saw, in the gloomy recesses, two gleaming eyes that reflected the light entering from the cavern's mouth. I did my best to make out the body but failed, since the gloom was too dense. I closed my eyes to listen, but the timeless stillness swallowed everything. All I could hear was my own breathing.

I was quiet for a time. When I reopened my eyes, I found that they had adjusted sufficiently to the darkness for me to see. The figure stood erect in a corner of the cave, as still as a stone statue. There was a weird, unfathomable gleam to its blazing eyes. It had curving horns like those of a Barbary ram, but its body was that of a gazelle, although of huge proportions. It was gazing at me with intense curiosity, but without moving, shying, or even breathing. It might just as well have been an empty hide. I picked up a small stone and tossed it at the creature, but it did not react, bolt, or take flight. I crept toward it on my hands and knees, narrowing the gap between us. Then I saw its pupils expand and enlarge as the strange gleam of its pupils became more intense. I kept staring, and a secret was awakened in my heart. A sharp odor assailed my nostrils, but I did not look away. I was afflicted by a strange trembling and the mysterious whispering spread to my heart. I deciphered in its eyes a prophetic message, which I read without difficulty, although it was wordless. Involuntarily, I mumbled a cryptic, incomprehensible phrase. I crawled out of the cave on all fours and then attempted to rise to my feet but failed. I was forced to continue crawling. I descended the cliff face, still on all fours. When I reached the base of the mountain, I lay quietly on my back and started to shake. The prophecy was making my head pound. As it matured, I felt dizzy and then nauseous. My heart was awash with whispered temptations, and I began to vomit. I threw up for a long time. Then I went into convulsions. I stroked my chest and found its covering soft to the touch and thick enough to arouse suspicions. When I investigated my leather clothing, I discovered that it adhered to my skin, like skin. I tried to strip it off, but how can you pull skin from skin? I cried out for help but heard only a choking rattle.

The composite apparition with the Barbary ram's head and gazelle's body showed me no mercy. It overtook me and stood over my head with its glittering, doubt-provoking eyes. I struggled against my despair and gazed into its eyes. The composite creature gazed right back. I continued staring. The dusky coloring of its eyes became ever more intense and they looked more mysterious. I did not budge while the mystery transmogrified. Once the mystery lifted, the prophecy's distinguishing features stood out more clearly. In the profound, unfamiliar talisman, I saw myself. The stone eyeball was transformed into the surface of water flowing from Heaven's spring, Salsabil, and I saw myself clearly in it. I saw I was a monster. I saw I was a freak. I saw I was a creature patched together from two disparate animals. I could not believe that I was still myself, and yet I felt certain my essence had not been destroyed. Only then was I freed. I could feel my body becoming liberated. I regained the ability to stand erect and found that I had the power to speed through the air.

2   Midday

THE POWER THAT ENABLED me to speed through the air helped me mingle with the herds, of which I became a member from that day on. In the lowlands I bounded with the gazelle fawns. I ascended mountain crags with the Barbary sheep kids. I nursed beside them, sucking milk from their mothers' teats, and we competed for the plants that grew on the plains and for the roots of vegetation on the mountain flanks. We shared the dates strewn beneath the palms. The intimidating gazelle with the horns of a Barbary ram had become a mother and father for me ever since the power spread through my heart the day we met in the cavern. She was a creature endowed with a gazelle's ability to traverse treacherous sandy plains and a Barbary sheep's ability to clamber up the highest mountain peaks. To attain the steep flanks of the southern mountain I would cling to her meager tail. I would climb on her back to reach the grazing lands of the sandy plains to the north, east, and west. I hung from her neck, swinging back and forth and amusing myself. I had forgotten. I had forgotten my mission. I did not brood about my true nature; I had even forgotten forgetting.

I do not know how long my exile lasted, but the whispered temptation returned one winter day, when the sky was veiled by gloomy, thick clouds and the mountain summits were shaken by a bombardment more ferocious than any I had ever heard in the desert. The herds fled and scattered. The flocks of Barbary sheep sought refuge in their mountains, and the herds of gazelles hid in the groves of palm trees. The thundering did not cease. The clouds started to shoot out terrifying bolts, and the heavens overhead were aflame with blinding fires. The herds grew increasingly alarmed and huddled together. I hid too. I had lost sight of my mother's tail and sought refuge with a herd of gazelles in a grove. I had squeezed in among them beneath a low palm with bushy fronds when the sky was rocked by such a terrifying roll of thunder that it seemed as if it would crash down and collapse on the face of the earth. Then I observed a gap languishing in the heavenly conflagration. This fissure was ablaze with flames and stretched forth a fiery tongue to strike the tops of the tallest palms, and so the grove began to catch fire. Smoke was everywhere, but my terror-stricken clan stuck together and did not budge or flee. I heard the agony of the palms' branches, which were caught by lapping fire, but did not catch their toasty scent until the top fronds began to fall on our miserable palm, which burst into flames as well.

The singular fragrance sparked the new prophecy in my heart and roused me, even though it seemed difficult, impossible even, to decipher the talisman. In my anxiety I began to shake. The whispered appeal apparently caused me so much pain that I rushed from the thicket into the fire. As the scorched smell in the air became more pungent, my sense of prophetic inspiration increased, but the prophecy itself did not pour forth. I shot off, racing across plains that were awash with the heaven's deluge, not knowing whether I was galloping to flee from the conflagration or in search of a stratagem that would illuminate the prophetic message inside me. Yet I never doubted that it was a smell that had excited me: the scents of the fire, of a body being consumed by fire, of mystery, of a prophetic maxim, and of greed. A ravenous appetite, which I could not account for, swept through my body, affecting me like a lethal poison, and I ran as if deranged. My flight carried me far away. I reached the grassy valleys that lie to the north and found them flooded by the heavenly downpour. I lapped the flood water, hoping to extinguish the coal flaming in my belly, but the water, which was created to give life, not to exterminate it, did not douse the flames. I retraced my steps and, without meaning to, returned to the burning palm groves. The herd had cleared out of their hiding place and scattered across the adjacent plain. The thunderous bombardment had ceased, the downpour was checked, dwindling to scattered drops, and the cloud cover had begun to break up, but the fire in the grove burned on. As I approached the palms, that scent grew stronger. I struggled with dizziness. I was trying not to succumb to it, when I observed, beneath the palm's burning trunk, a wretched, young ewe's body consumed by flames. Smoke rose from what was left of her corpse. I took another step closer to poke this mound. A repulsive liquid like blood, purulence, or pus flowed out, escaping from the body. I took a stick and scraped charred lumps off her rump. The flesh had been blackened by flames, which had reduced it to bits and pieces, even as smoke continued to rise from some areas. When I plunged the stick into the creature's thigh, the smoke subsided and the steamy scent wafted from it; the appetizing aroma of the scent that had driven me crazy. I began to tremble once more. So, without any premeditation, I stretched out my hand and feverishly pulled a chunk off the thigh. With my teeth, I tore into the flesh, which—although charred and saturated with blood and dirt—released an appetizing vapor. I savored it thoroughly, bit into the chunk, and began to chew it with the voracity of a sick man. The morsel dissolved in my mouth, and my saliva mixed with the blood, charred flesh, and mud. Then my limbs relaxed, my trembling ceased, and my fever lifted. Calm flowed through my body. Once I consumed the antidote, I heard a supernatural whisper, which was the catalyst for a weird sensation that was a forgotten prophecy.

The fog finally dispersed, and the vision's details became clear. I saw a boy rolling between two full breasts before dropping into a dark abyss. I had to struggle even longer to make out the character of the abyss, which was that obscure ghost I today call "forgetfulness," before I could perceive the cure—memory. It helped me remember my name.

After I recovered my name, the gloom lifted and the dream vision continued, starting with the rituals of childbirth and ending with the hunting knife I used to sever my father's sway over me.

A new, profound sensation took hold of me. It rocked me, but I only recognized it much later as that murky enigma the tribes refer to as "happiness." I did not then know that the spirit world, which grants happiness, normally refuses to grant it unalloyed. In my case, when I used the stick to poke at the ewe's body roasted by the fire, I discovered, in part of the body buried under the heap, the twin, curved horns from the head of the creature that was a composite of a Barbary ram and a gazelle. Then I realized that I had poisoned my body with "evil," since I had devoured my mother's flesh, which had been molded together with my father's.

3   Afternoon

THE CLOUDS LIFTED and the sky lost its distinguishing features, but the earth remained soaked from the downpour. I plunged into the mires in the valleys to rejoin the herds. I saw a knot of gazelles in the northern plains, but they shied away from me. I moved a few steps closer, but they looked alarmed, prepared to flee, and stamped the earth with their hooves. When I advanced still farther, they shot off all together, as if fleeing from a jackal. I rushed off too and caught up with them before I knew it, but the herd continued to flee and disappeared behind the hills that lead to the eastern ridges of sand. I raced after them for a long way. I gave chase, because the flight by this herd of my boon companions awakened in my heart an ugly feeling of abandonment. I choked on a bitterness that clouded my happiness by immediately bringing back my memory. I felt as ostracized, deserted, and banished as the day I fled from my tribe's encampment. When I pondered the secret behind the gazelles' rejection, I could think of nothing save my gluttony. Had the appetizing morsel constituted an act of civil disobedience grave enough to warrant my banishment? Was I destined to become an alien again because of this ill-omened slip? Had the gazelle clans welcomed me only because forgetfulness had allowed me to revert to a swaddling-clothes stage of animal metamorphosis and to morph into a gazelle or a Barbary sheep without my realizing it, and had this stage lasted until I devoured the morsel and thus freed myself from it by regaining my memory, only to have my shameful identity revealed to the herds, which then fled from me, horrified by my true nature? Was it reasonable for that era to end and for me to be denied forgiveness, just because I ate the flesh of a relative—not out of hunger but driven by the intoxication of something I later learned is called "greed"? All the same, I did not admit defeat.

I crossed over the northern hills to circle back on the herd from the spines of sand, but the mires slowed my pace. I did not reach the lower valleys until late that afternoon. The sky had cleared, although the shells of a few clouds loitered in the void. In the valleys, moist vapors continued to rise, carrying to my nostrils the earth's prophetic counsel. Looking down over the depression below me, I spotted the herd grazing in its hollow. I fell to my knees and watched from my vantage point.

The gazelles were roaming peacefully, munching on plants as dry as chaff down to their roots, since they had appealed for sustenance to an earth reduced to powder by the intense drought. The gazelles lowered their heads to pluck at the stalks and then began to glance around nervously, as if sensing danger. They turned to the right and left and kept flicking their tails, another sign they thought danger was nigh.

Some of the fawns bounded hither and yon, while others were busy drawing milk from their mothers' teats. Males with horns haughtily patrolled the circumference, not stooping to nibble the grass. Instead, they stood guard over the herd, earnestly endeavoring to protect it. I watched a male that kept staring at my hill, as if he had found me out. Then I saw the prophecy in his eyes, despite his arrogance. I saw the prophetic message in his stance, physique, build, coloring, posture, nobility, and in his eyes, which gazed into the void of eternity, staring at the spirit world, which I could not see. Was it beauty? Was this the beauty that had disowned me and was too hardhearted to pardon me? How could I live without beauty? How could beauty be retrieved?

I crept on all fours across the top of the hill and continued in the same fashion down its flank. I approached the nearest doe and gazed into her eyes. She stared back at me, stopped chewing, and stamped the earth with her hoof. I used my eyes to show her my affection. I entreated her with my eyes. I told her I was the same creature who had played with her the day before and who had shared her hiding place this very day, but she rejected me. She kicked the ground with her front hoof. Then she bolted, and the herd bolted with her. They shot off like an arrow in the air and vanished from sight. This was how I realized that my tie to the herd had been severed. I admitted to myself that I had not merely lost beauty but had emerged as beauty's eternal foe. Still, I did not capitulate.

I left the gazelles, resolving to try my luck with the nation of Barbary sheep. I galloped across the ravine, traversed the valleys, and then plunged into the muddy wallows of the plains, as if pursued by a demon from the spirit world. I fell many times, and my feet sank into the mud up to my knees. I do not know how I reached the bare, rocky area adjacent to the southern mountain's cliff face, which was cloaked by sandy deposits that twisted like serpents' bodies. Apparently my struggle through the mires had transformed me into a monster uglier than any other, for the sight of me caused the herds of Barbary sheep to bolt from the mountain's foot and to gallop en masse uphill. I scaled the cliff face behind them, as if possessed, and did not slow my pace until I caught up with a pregnant ewe, whose progress was hampered by the creature she bore in her belly. As she raced higher, she stepped on a friable layer of rock that time had weakened. Her two rear hooves slipped so that her belly hit the ground, and she began to slide back. She attempted to stop her fall with her front hooves but failed. Then she tried to save herself with her head, planting her muzzle in crevices between brittle layers of stone, but she could not hold on and continued to slide ever lower in a slow, grievous descent. I reached her, or more precisely she reached me, for her descent rather than my effort to catch her placed her before me. I seized her rear hoof, gasping to catch my breath, but she stamped her hoof in a murderous way to free herself. I recklessly grabbed hold of her hoof with both hands. She was quiet then only because she was too weak to resist, not because she felt reassured. She turned her head toward me, and in her eyes I perceived not only dust, mucous, and grains of sand but terror, revulsion, and agony.

I was so hurt by the agony visible in her weeping eyes that a tear sprang from my eye too. I massaged her body, which was shaking violently. Seeking a way to regain her trust, I whispered to her, in Tuareg, "It's me. Have you forgotten me?"

Her response, however, was a rude kick to my right cheek. Then she struggled to break free. She succeeded and began bravely climbing higher, but the eroding layers of rock failed her once more, and she slid back down to find herself in my grasp again. Then she bleated desperately before turning toward me. I could read in her eyes a plea and an admission of impotence. She collapsed on her right side and gazed at me in despair. I stroked her neck to reassure her but noticed that her misery continued to show in her eyes. She was allowing me to touch her only because she was too weak to resist, not because she liked me. I wondered what secret had separated me from these docile creatures, which only the day before had been my family, my race, and my clan. The only answer I could find to this puzzle was the hunk of meat. Had I been transformed, in one fell swoop, into a predator in their eyes? Was I a monster that had denied his true nature by swallowing the morsel and had then become a different creature that deserved to be shunned?

The sheets of crumbling rock collapsed under our combined weight, and we tumbled downhill. I found myself hugging her body with both hands as we fell. I put my arms around her neck, which I pressed against mine. I sensed the moisture of her snot on my face, her breathing in my ear, her heartbeats in my heart, and the pulsing fetus in her belly with my pulse. We were united during our descent, for I felt she was part of me and I part of her. I regained my sense of wellbeing and composure, since I had regained my feeling of affiliation.

The rocks scraped my skin grievously, and I bled profusely. I did not feel the pain, however, until some time after we landed. The trip down did not take long, but it was long enough for that emotion I learned priests call "happiness" to be sparked for a few moments in my soul. This flighty emotion does not tarry with us long. A boulder blocked our path and brought us to a halt. When we came to a stop, our union terminated and a painful estrangement ensued. Our bodies separated, and exile reasserted its sovereignty over my world. The ewe kicked me in the chest with her two front hooves and forced me, against my will, to release my hold on her neck. She shook herself free and rose to her four feet to confront me. She panted. From her nostrils she discharged dust, mixed with drops of the snot that had spattered over me. She glared at my face. She stared at my eyes, at my pupils, and at whatever lay behind my pupils. She saw, or so it seemed, everything in my eyes. The slow deliberation with which she backed away revealed her terror, alarm, and revulsion. Without meaning to, I crawled toward her. I crept after her to reclaim her. I crawled toward her to restore our harmony and to recreate our bond. I stretched out my hand, both my hands, as if begging, but she backed away from me with a strange zeal, never ceasing to stare at my eyes with that terrifying look.

I trailed after her. I found myself pulled toward her. I could not bear to be separated from her. I could not stand to be parted from her. She continued to retreat. She backed until a boulder blocked her from the rear. Her pupils narrowed. She was swept by a fear greater than any I had ever witnessed. It was a mixture of despair, grief, and impotence. When she opened her eyes, a liquid flowed from them. I saw it glide down her muzzle till drops fell on the rocks of the cliff face. She closed her eyes and began to tremble once more. She shook violently before reopening them. Then I detected a new gleam, a different one, a look of genuine determination and of the courage a creature feels when it decides to terminate a problem and to be heroic. Then . . . suddenly, she sprang. She shot toward me in a lethal leap, which I dodged only at the last second, by tumbling over backwards. Then I saw her bound into the air and disappear behind the boulder. Before I came to terms with what had happened I heard the heavy crash of her body against the earth. Leaping up, I discovered that only the boulder that had stopped our descent had prevented our conjoined bodies from falling into an abyss. My eyes searched for her from my lofty perch but could not make her out among the rocks below. I bounded down the cliff face, although my progress was hampered by rocks I repeatedly had to sidestep. Eventually I tripped over a stone, fell to the ground, and began to roll down the hill. I tumbled a long way. I tumbled the whole way down till I reached the chasm's floor. My limbs were bathed in blood, but I felt numb all over. As I stood above her body, I saw that, although she was still breathing, she was dying. Her swollen belly rose and fell. Blood trickled from her muzzle and flowed over the rocks of the pit.

Blood also spouted from her rump. She bellowed profoundly while the sides of her abdomen stretched taut and contracted. She discharged a lot of mucous and blood, before discharging the fetus in one fell swoop.

I rushed to the newborn and took it in my hands. It was limp and slimy with blood, amniotic fluid, and threads of mucous. Its eyes were covered by a veil as diaphanous as spiders' webs. The eye beneath the coating was extinguished. The lamb quivered in my hands once and then a second time before it subsided, forever.

The mother also quivered as she released her final breath at exactly the same moment.

4   Evening

I HEADED FOR THE CAVERN decorated with the wisdom of the ancients and spent several days there. I did not feel like eating and was disgusted by everything, even the hunk of meat that had sparked greed in my heart the day lightning incinerated the ewe formed from the body of a gazelle and the head of a Barbary ram.

Whenever I recalled that taste, I saw in my mind the image of the Barbary ewe that had fled from me forcing from her body her stillborn lamb—a-swirl in fluids—and her last breaths. Then I was unable to keep myself from vomiting till I almost spat out my guts. My only consolation came from kneeling to beg for forgiveness beneath the images that the ancestors' shamans had traced on the hard walls. I brooded about my situation for two days following the death of the ewe and her lamb. The only cure I could devise was to admit the truth. After a prolonged internal debate, I realized that all along the source of my conflict with the herds had not been, as I had originally tried to persuade myself, my conquest of beauty, but my seizure of prey capable of quieting gluttony's call in my belly. Yes, greed was the cause. The gluttony revealed by my consumption of the ill-omened morsel had not only poisoned my body but had stripped me of my camouflage as a member of the herds. That was the cause. So how could I free myself of these poisons and absolve myself of my error?

Yet, it seemed my hunger for meat turned out to be the stronger drive, for my feelings of nausea eventually disappeared, and the image of the ewe and her newborn also faded away, so that I found myself, without any conscious decision, prowling around the herds' grazing lands once again. I prowled there for a long time without bagging a victim from either species and was finally reduced to employing a different type of amulet, one I dubbed *iyghf* or "reasoning."

I brought fresh palm stalks from the groves and began to plait them into a circular form. By trimming away the leaves, I created a perfect circle. Then I crisscrossed the heart of the circle with rows of twigs that I fastened to the circular frame by threads of bast. I called this base fabrication *tasarsamt* or "trap." After that, I headed to the pasture where I dug a pit as deep as I could reach and then placed my ignoble handiwork exactly over the mouth of the hole. I spread dry material and plants over the contraption so that it was invisible. Inspecting what my hands had wrought, I found it excellent. Then I retreated to a nearby acacia to relax as a reward for the effort I had taken to craft this excellent device. I rested under this bushy acacia and began to dream of the antidote that had restored my memory until—I do not know how or when—I dozed off.

I slept profoundly and did not wake until dawn had traced its talisman across the horizon. I went back down to the plain but found neither snare nor victim. I searched the area excitedly and discovered near the hole's mouth some fur tufts that convinced me the prey that had run off with my snare was a gazelle. I followed the tracks through depressions that twisted around before leading to the northeastern valleys. I descended into the low-lying valley bottoms, but their sides soon began to climb and rise to become, in the tracts beyond, trails that would ascend the peaks of the stubborn sand ridges. In the muddy valley bottoms I could see the track much more clearly. My victim had circled an acacia tree repeatedly, as if appealing to it for help in liberating herself from her shackle, but the tree had snagged her body in the form of bits of furry hide stuck to thorns. At a steep bend, where the ravine rose stubbornly to join gullies that came down from the highest reaches, I found blood on smooth rocks that crowded together at the mouth of the ravine like a thicket of boulders.

I darted over their smooth tops, which were rounded like the tombs of ancients in the northern desert. Here I lost the track but found it again after I had left the stone thicket and the trail became easier, less challenging, and higher. In this easy stretch, the shrubs fell away to the rear to disappear among the lower rocks, fleeing from the vanguards of the sandy rebel. In this area, only some low-lying plants blanketed the earth, seeking refuge from the fiery sky with the sun-baked surface of the aggressive ridges of sand. The track was clearer on the sandy soil. It seemed that my victim had risked her life attempting to free herself from the snare, for the struggle waged over this interval had resulted in heavy bleeding and in her shedding tufts of blood-soaked fur. Then, suddenly, the track disappeared. I retraced my steps to scout the area where the trail forked into two gullies. I followed the gulley that turned off toward the east without finding any tracks there. I stopped to peer around. I looked to the south and the north. I spotted her. I saw her with my heart before I noticed her with my eyes. I sensed her presence before I caught sight of her. Had it not been for this strange sensation, I would not have retraced my steps. I would not have explored the second gulley. I would not have paused at this spot rather than another. I would not have peered to the south and the north only to espy her hidden in a pit located between the two trails. A dense bramble of dry, interwoven branches hid her

from view. The snare that I had laid over the hole played a part
in concealing her. She was trembling violently from fear and
pain, and snot was streaming from her muzzle. From the leg held
by the teeth of the trap flowed fresh blood, which was mingled
with clots of dry dirt. The silent call that had guided me back to
her had been prophetic, for when I seized hold of her, I discovered that her leg had worked free from the snare and that its
teeth no longer grasped anything save a hoof, so the doe would
definitely have freed herself had she bolted from her hiding
place. As I grasped hold of her with two quivering hands her
trembling became even more violent.

Her eyes flashed with fear, innocence, despair, and beauty. I
embraced her with both arms and hugged her to my chest, without knowing why. Perhaps the look in her wide, dark eyes was
irresistible. Perhaps it was because the prophecy I detected in
her deep eyes would never be repeated. Perhaps it was because
the significance I read in the flash of her eyes was as intimate as
it was painful, so that anxiety prevented me from discovering
the secret of either our intimacy or her pain, because the call of
greed suppressed the voice of truth in my heart. I did not hear it
until after I had slaughtered her with a sharp stone, skinned,
and eaten her.

Once her death cry fell silent, that voice grew louder.
Anxiety was dissipated, the gloom faded, and the mysteries were
revealed. I heard the statement her eyes had addressed to me in
that look. Inspiration burst forth, and I recognized in the
gazelle's eyes the mother who had twice rescued me from
destruction: once when wicked denizens of the spirit world,
masquerading as the hare of misfortune, had enticed me and
caused me to lose my way when I was searching for my father,
and a second time when the world collapsed around me the day
I slaughtered my father with a hunting knife only to find myself

alone, abandoned, banished, a pariah. My situation in short had been tantamount to Anubi's. My mother had arrived, thrust me into her skin, and fled far away to save me yet another time through metamorphosis.

5   Dusk

WITH THIS BLOODY ESCAPADE commenced my break with the herds. Thereafter my animal kin shunned me and braved the heights to cross over into unknown realms.

The gazelles migrated to the north, crossing lofty, sand-strewn peaks to cast themselves into the mighty sea of sand. The Barbary sheep clans migrated to the south, scaling the circle of southern mountains and crossing into the trackless deserts that lead to mountain chains with surging peaks, about which the tribes recount fantastic legends as part of epics handed down from their forefathers. I first followed the gazelles' trail in their journey northward but then retraced my steps rather than tackle the sandy slope that cast me down to the oasis one day, for I remembered that gazelles are a species extraordinarily hard to capture when traversing sandy ground. I conjectured, on the other hand, that I could catch up with the herds of Barbary sheep, which are slow creatures on the difficult plains that dot the southern desert before it reaches the mountain chains of whose impregnable heights fantastic legends are narrated. The hope for escape for Barbary sheep is always weaker when they enter a sandy area. The hope for escape for gazelles, conversely, is weaker when they enter mountainous terrain, as time-honored proverbs assert.

I scaled the mountain but had trouble ascending the highest boulders leading to the summit. So I fell back on my wits and sought easier passageways through the chain's westward extension. That took me the whole day, and dusk fell before I discovered a gap. As darkness overtook me, I cast about for a sheltered place where I could spend the night. Stretching out in a hollow at the base of a column-like boulder, which was suggestive in its majesty of an idol, I surveyed from my lofty perch the low-lying areas where my oasis looked a modest plot no different from the groves of acacia or retem in some of the valleys of the northern desert. When I cast my eyes upwards, the bare, dispassionate sky spoke to me in a stern tongue. As it addressed me, I pondered the cause for the temporary insanity that drove me to pursue creatures that shunned me. Had gluttony motivated me to chase after them? Was gluttony an illness, a need, or an appetite? Was I pursuing them and risking my life in their pursuit out of a longing to capture beauty, which for some unknown reason I felt I could not live without? Was my pursuit motivated by fear of solitude? Was my pursuit occasioned by some other unknown cause? Was I pursuing because man must always pursue, so that even when he finds nothing to pursue, he invents a prey, albeit fictitious, deceptive, or imaginary? Was I pursuing them merely out of stubbornness, because these creatures that had so recently constituted my kin had banished me from their ranks in the course of one day, leaving me a fugitive, alone, and shunned, so that I resembled no one so much as a bastard, desert Anubi? Or did my motivation actually lurk deep within a whispering appeal that told me this rejection was not a rejection but a portent embracing an awe-inspiring truth related to my truth, which no stratagem had allowed me to discern in myself?

I wondered and wondered until my head hurt so much it was ready to burst open. Sleep carried me off before I could reach any answer to any question. I awoke to a dawn that was still cloaked in darkness. I sped away at that early hour, acting on

the counsel of the Barbary sheep community, which recom-
mends: "Travel in the morning, rising at dawn, in order to reach
your destination."

I struggled past the stone monoliths until dawn receded and
a firebrand was born on the horizon. I climbed a forbidding cliff
face and found I was ascending the mountain's summit from its
western side. Because of the gloom, I was not able to discern the
full extension of its foothills. I groped my way through a rela-
tively easy opening but was unable to make out the lay of the
land until the darkness was routed and light prevailed. The
region was filled with mountainous knobs of gloomy hue and
modest elevation. These were spaced out and scattered at some
points and, in other locations smack dab together. They rose at
times and fell in other places till the plains terminated them.
All the same, their average height remained constant, even
though they were paralleled at the rear by true mountain peaks.
Thus the oasis at the bottom appeared to be in a pit rather than
on a plain.

I discovered dung from Barbary sheep on the sandy blazon
encircling the haunch of one of these knobs. When I rubbed it
between my fingers, I found it was still fresh, but the ewe's trail
disappeared where the sandy band terminated. So I made for the
heights, knowing that Barbary sheep would typically be satisfied
with no other type of refuge. I persevered till midday without
finding a single ewe. My throat was parched, my tongue and lips
were dry, and my body had shed its sweat reserve. I saw that I
had forsaken sound counsel when I failed to respond to the
inner voice that had advised me all along to desist and turn
back before it was too late. I searched for a shrub or boulder that
would afford me some shade until the noonday heat passed, but
the soil was of that grievous type the tribes say was cursed at
some time; a fiery heat emerging from the center of the desert

had scorched it, wiping out all vegetation until even plant seeds had disappeared. The only crop its dirt produced was stones.

I resolved to turn back but thought I would never survive unless I found a place where I could shelter from the siesta-time heat. I committed another error for once again I ignored the little voice and went forward, hoping to run across some shade behind the hill, which was bathed by waves of mirages.

I pressed forward, but the hill retreated ever farther away the more I advanced toward it, as if fleeing from me. I remembered the tricks mirages play in the northern desert and felt certain that I had fallen out of the pan into the fire and that confusion had once again led me into harm's way. My vision was blurred, and I started to see double. My body shook from a weakness that struck without warning. I felt dizzy, dropped to my knees in a grim, eternal solitude, with a scorching earth beneath me and a furnace overhead. Only then did I understand that my crime lay not in venturing farther into the desert than I should have, but in entering the desert in search of anything other than water. I realized at last that although the fates had provided me with everything I needed, I had rebelled and set forth in search of something I had never needed. I deserved the fury and punishment of the sun-baked earth.

I perceived clearly that a sip of water was all I needed. Why had I disdained the bold stream, the springs, and life in general to set out like a madman in search of a figment of the imagination and a lie, substituting for life a shadow of life? Now I had landed myself in life-threatening isolation, where I was searching for a drop of moisture in a rocky desert. I did not even dare to think about the copious supply of water I had left behind, since all I dreamt of was some shade to shelter me from the blazing sky and to preserve in my body all of the lost treasure I could salvage.

I crawled for a distance, but the scorching earth burned my hands. I licked them and fell on my stomach and elbows. I began to wriggle forward on my belly like a snake but was not able to wriggle far. I lay on my back. My face was burned by the punishing sun and my back by the punishing earth. I burned until I no longer felt the inferno. I sensed I was about to pass out. I do not know how long I was unconscious, but the sip of water that saved my life certainly preceded the prophecy I heard from the mouth of the emissary who stood above my head: "It is not wise to neglect what we have in order to search for what we lack."

He placed the mouth of his water-skin in my mouth, and the water poured down my throat. I could feel it flow through my body and spread into my blood, restoring my faculties to me. I regained the ability to use my hands and grasped the water-skin with thirst's insanity, attempting to empty it into my belly in one gulp, but the emissary seized it, pulling it away from my mouth. "This is the answer," he said. "This is the secret. It is all about greed."

I was thirsty. I had returned in an instant from a trip to the unknown. My dream was to provision myself with more of the antidote that had rescued me from the ghoul's grip. I made a sign with my eyes. I begged with my eyes, because—like others who have fallen into the ghoul's grip and then miraculously returned to the desert of the living—I had lost the ability to speak. Even so, the apparition kept the water-skin out of my reach while he proclaimed sagely: "You had a comfortable living bestowed on you, but you betrayed your covenant."

My tongue, however, stammered with the wisdom of the thirsty: "Water!"

"You received water and betrayed it by setting out on a journey. Where are you heading? Where?"

"Give me a sip, and I'll tell you a secret."

"No one who has disavowed his secret has a secret."

"Did I disavow my secret by setting forth in search of food?"

"We provided you with the fruit of the palm for nourishment. So don't lie."

"Dates are a lifeless form of nourishment."

"Lifeless?"

"Any nourishment devoid of that riddle named beauty is lifeless food."

"Beauty is a treasure that gives life, not a deadly ordeal."

"How can one seize beauty, master?"

"Beauty always evades us if we set out to search for it."

"Master, I have never dreamt of obtaining anything so much as I've dreamt of obtaining beauty. When, however, I departed one day to search for my father, I lost my way and was not destined to return, for I found myself stuffed into the jug of metamorphoses."

"Do you see? This was your punishment. You should not search for anything you do not find in your heart. You are beauty. You are your father. You are prophecy. You are the treasure!"

He chanted his words as if reciting verse. He swayed right and left, as if in a trance. He uttered groans of pain reminiscent of those of people overcome by longing. My faculties were restored and life began to pulse through my body. I said, "I gave up searching for my father one day and decided to look for Targa, but the spirit world cast me into an oasis whose name I don't even know."

"What the spirit world wishes for us is always nobler than what we wish for ourselves."

"I don't understand."

"The oasis whose name you don't know is real, but Targa is a false illusion."

"I don't understand."

"Targa too is a lost oasis."

"I've heard members of my tribe speak of caravans that left for Targa."

"Caravans that leave for Targa don't return. It is the lost caravans that head for Targa."

"Targa is lost, the law is a lost set of prophetic admonitions, and the people of the desert are a lost tribe. Are we, then, bastard children of heaven like Anubi?"

"Each one of us is Anubi; each a fleeting shadow."

"But . . . who are you?"

"I am a fleeting shadow."

Because of my fatigue, dizziness, and ordeal-induced daze, I was not able to make out his features clearly, but sparks in my heart tried to tell me something. "Has the spirit world not brought us together before?" I asked.

He stuck to his enigmatic response: "I'm naught but a fleeting shadow."

The sparks in my heart illuminated a corner veiled by darkness, and I pulled myself together and struggled onto my elbows. I clung to his blue veil, which gleamed indigo in the twilight. Unaware of what I was doing, I shouted, "Not so fast! You are my father! Are you my father?"

He stared at my face for a time. His eyes narrowed to slits, but when he opened them again I detected an attractive smile in them, the smile of a child who has received what he wants. I struggled against vertigo once more but heard his prophetic admonition clearly: "What need for a father has one whose father is the heavens?"

"I heard a maxim saying that a father is the antidote for misery and that a creature who has never discovered his father will never be happy. So, who are you?"

He continued to gaze silently at me. The childish smile in his eyes twinkled brighter and became more affectionate and tender. I smiled too, for I sensed intuitively that he was preparing to give me some good news. I wished he would be quick to quench my thirst for the truth before my heart grew confused and I passed out again. He, however, took his time, deliberately I supposed. Just when I felt the whispered onset of unconsciousness I heard him say: "I'm you!"

6   After Midnight

"THE PROPHET OF EXPLORATION guided us," said the first strangers when they reached my oasis. I hurried out to greet them before I could mask my astonishment. Once they had descended through the pass between the sandy mountains of the west and the rocky ones of the south, I asked: "Who are you?"

The elder leading them replied: "Wanderers parched by thirst."

"How did you cross the rocky wastes to reach here?"

"The prophet of exploration guided us."

"Amazing!"

"Please postpone your amazement till later and give us water from your spring."

I led them to the nearest of my four groves, and they knelt to sip from the spring. They thrust their mouths into the deluge till their noses and faces disappeared. Their animals also darted to the bubbling waters. I stood beside them, waiting until they had slaked their thirst. I watched the delight they took in the water, till thirst stirred in my heart too. This was the thirst concealed, since birth, in the psyche of every desert dweller, for it can never be quenched, even if he consumes all the water in the world. Awakened in my heart was the thirst that had become an enigmatic murmur ever since I was overcome by thirst while searching for the Barbary sheep. Unlike the spirit world's emissary, who wrested the water-skin from my mouth that day, I did not drive these people from the water but, rather, found myself also dropping to my knees to sip from the bubbling water. I sipped and only came to my senses when the caravan's leader repeated less than grammatically, "Four! Four! Not just one well, but they is four. What have you done for spirit world that grant you four treasures?"

I replied with the stupidity of one who has been isolated from other people for a long time and who has forgotten the niceties of expression: "I didn't do anything. I was searching for my father."

He gazed into my eyes for a long time. Then he looked away, toward the peaks of the southern mountains; over the peaks in fact, for he stared upward. His eyes shone with a look of longing. His chest growled nervously, and he swayed like someone in an ecstatic trance before proclaiming, "No one else is compensated like a person who demonstrates how to search for a father."

"But I killed him."

"What?"

"The she-jinni said I killed my father."

He hummed with suppressed longing once more and allowed his eyes to roam the naked, eternal emptiness. His distress set his shoulders to shaking. The look of his eyes changed into real tears. He repeated, "No, no. You didn't kill your father! You can't kill your father. You slew a shadow and found your father. Believe me!"

Then he turned to his vassals and ordered them to fetch gifts: dried meats, clothes, skins, containers, and many other objects, the uses of which I only grasped later. As he piled these items at my feet, he declared, "You must have suffered a great deal."

"I don't understand."

"Only those who suffer succeed. All my gifts to you count as nothing compared to what you have given me. Your gift has granted me life. Your gift will continue to afford life."

I was going to object, but he stopped me with a gesture of his hand. "These meats are from creatures that will safeguard you from the meat of relatives."

"The meat of relatives?"

"The prophet who guided us to you told me everything."

"I don't understand."

"The prophet said you had set out to search for relatives but had almost perished from dehydration."

"I went out in search of beauty."

"Beauty? Did you kill beauty?"

"The thirst for beauty, master, is worse than the thirst for water."

"But beauty's not beautiful unless we touch it. Beauty's not beautiful unless it touches us. Beauty's not beautiful unless we envelope it and it envelopes us the way metamorphosis envelopes composite creatures."

He turned to his vassals and ordered them to fetch two animals from the caravan. Placing their halters in my hand, he said, "This is a male camel and this a female. You will use them to help you bear the burdens of your world."

He passed the night in my shelter. In the morning, he provisioned himself with water, loaded his goods onto the camels, and set off after embracing me and chanting for me a plaintive, passionate song of longing. I kept repeating it to myself so I could comfort myself with it in my solitary times.

7   Daybreak

THE SIGHT OF THE TWO CAMELS freely roaming the plains, as their bodies vanished up to their chests in grass the desert had generously offered, after being irrigated by the heavy, recent downpours, stirred in my soul happiness of the rare species that we can experience but fail to verbalize when we try. The mystery of this sensation frequently left me wondering whether its cause was the sight of the two beasts of burden, the vision of the lush grass, the temperate weather, my carefree existence, or the conjunction of all these blessings. I can testify that the sensation not only appeared suddenly but proved evanescent and ephemeral whenever I attempted to appropriate and detain it, to enjoy it longer. My subsequent disappointment was always bitter. Is happiness a vibratory hum that pervades us only while it is far from our thoughts, so that once we perceive it and attempt to grasp hold, it slips through our fingers and flees far away?

I attempted to outwit happiness so that I could hold onto it. One stratagem I tried was to pretend not to notice it, hoping in this way to ensnare it miraculously. Then I discovered that this beloved does not desire us if we desire it and does not yearn for us unless we choose some rival beloved. I would have to forget it, or to pretend to forget it, to bring off my miracle. I made a pet of the she-camel and fondled her in the animal

yard each morning before I took her to the grazing lands. I
would pluck bloodsucking ticks from her neck and clear away
the stalks of straw that adhered to her hump, belly, and thighs.
I would dress with herbal salves the wounds that thorns had
torn in her flesh while she was craning her neck in the palm
groves. I noticed that she enjoyed the feel of my fingers moving over her body even more than being liberated from the
ticks, thorns, or straw. Soon I began to multiply my caresses
and prolong my massages down her body, endeavoring with my
fingers to express my affection and anxiety or even longing, so
that she would be forced to respond. At first she fidgeted and
shuddered slightly, as if importunate armies of flies had swept
down upon her, for all camels shake their coats in self-defense
then. Even so, this quivering of the skin was soon followed by
a disquieting ardor. She would rock her long, white neck to
the right and left, rearing it up. Her large, dark eyes would
gleam like those of my darling gazelles, and then she would
emit a profound, restrained, intermittent moan that left me
wondering whether it was a complaint, an intimate aside, or
an ecstatic cry. Then she would lower her neck till it rubbed
my shoulder, hand, or face. With her snout, which was damp
with froth, she would nuzzle my arms, fingers, nose, or head,
not ceasing until I did. I once attempted to groom as well her
mate, the male camel, of his ticks, thorns, and straw, but she
avenged herself on me, deserting me until I stretched out to
take a siesta under an acacia. Then she snuck up and stood
towering over my head. When I awoke I found her standing
there, her head stretched toward the horizon, which was limited solely by the sandy dunes north of the oasis.

    She was breathing heavily and chewing moodily, as if brood-
ing. Despair, anxiety, and malice were visible in her eyes. I
stretched out my hand to stroke her front leg, but she pulled it

away and thumped her chest a mighty blow. I drew myself up on my elbows, but she did not soften toward me. I was caught off-guard when she jumped in the air to begin pummeling me with her feet. She hit my head, my right shoulder, and my left knee, and had I not sheltered myself by the acacia's trunk, I would not have escaped her mischief. I was obliged, in order to mollify her, to massage her body with both hands: once in the animal yard in the morning, a second time out in the grazing lands at mid-day, and a third time back in the yard in the evening.

This relationship was not destined to last long, however, for the leader of a caravan, wishing to lavish gifts on me out of appreciation for the water, deposited a woman beside me, saying that he had purchased her in the forest lands and had decided to leave her in my custody to assist me with my daily chores. She was of mixed race, a skittish, comely, jumpy, excessively wary creature, who seemed ready to flee or to pounce. I soon had to acknowledge that she had awakened in my heart the whispers I had forgotten since the spirit world separated me from my lost she-jinni from whom I once learned some things. So it was not long before I was searching for my forgotten reality in this new creature's embrace, which did not bring me happiness. The new she-jinni did not trust me, despite her pretence at amiability. I observed how skeptical of me she remained over the course of the following days. I do not deny that I occasionally had pleasure with her, but I could not claim it was fully satisfying. Because she lacked the kind of beauty I had lost when I lost the gazelles, this pleasure was lackluster. In the beginning, I suspected that her indifference, skittishness, and wariness were symptoms of fear, perhaps a result of a longing for the solitude to which she was accustomed in her forest land. Subsequently I discovered that these characteristics were to the contrary a hankering to be close to other people and a desire for contact with villages. So she awakened in me my old sense of being an orphan, of solitude, and of being at my wits' end. Then I punished her by avoiding her. I acted condescending and holed up in the caverns of the ancestors for two consecutive nights. I abandoned her, feigning disdain for her gifts. The truth was, however, that I was not as liberated from the suzerainty of her embraces as I had imagined, for whispered temptations troubled me both nights I spent in the caves of the southern cliff faces more than at any time before. I realized that this she-jinni had soothed me more than anyone I had ever known before. So I hastened to rejoin her as soon as I saw her at the edge of the wadi, after I had descended the mountain on my return to the oasis. Yet I pretended not to see her and went to pet the she-camel at the bottom of the valley, because I have discovered that a creature who thirsts for the beauty he once found with gazelles is fated to recapture his dream only with she-camels, whose eyes flash with the gazelles' spirit.

I petted the she-camel, and the she-jinni stealthily trailed after me. I chanted to my gentle creature a song of longing, and my beloved grunted her pain and shared her suppressed sorrow with me. Despite preoccupation with this intimate conversation and despite being lost in the world of song, I was aware that the she-jinni was pursuing me. She disappeared behind a low hill separating the cliff face from the valley bottom. My beloved camel thrust her long neck against my chest, and I embraced her. I whispered to her that I loved her because she bore in her eyes the look of another beloved creature that had carried me in her body when I was on the point of perishing of thirst and had also returned to bear me once more the day I lost my father and my truth. The poor creature moaned in distress and swayed from right to left like an ecstatic religious celebrant overwhelmed by grief. The she-jinni, whom I had forgotten in my crazed dance, then ruined everything by suddenly popping up, as she-jinnis will. The beloved camel beside me took fright and bolted.

The she-camel fled, and I found myself standing face-to-face with a creature far more hideous than the she-jinni, one more like a she-demon. I forced myself to smile at her, but the evil look I saw in her eyes frightened me. So I retreated, but she did not approach me. She glared maliciously at me and then departed. She climbed the hill and vanished at a curve in the valley, where it stretched northward.

I tried to forget, but the whispered temptations would not cease. These frightened me more than the threat in her eyes, because I knew that such a threat is generally an empty one, whereas an *idée fixe* is nothing more or less than a prophecy. It seems that what I had learned was confirmed on this occasion as well, because I discovered beauty's paragon dead the next morning. I did not for a moment doubt that the she-jinni had plotted this outrage. I found the she-camel in the animal yard, all swollen up, her eyeballs protruding, with suspicious-looking snot oozing from her nostrils. I was certain that the she-jinni had given the camel poison mixed with dry grass. I pursued her to rebuke her for her deed, but she bared her teeth at me like a jackal and then pelted me with a hail of abuse in the forest dwellers' gibberish. So I left her and went off by myself to the open spaces to seek inspiration for some wily subterfuge. I told myself that a creature who plots the destruction of a fellow creature is a past-master of evil who will stop at nothing and that unless I succeeded in limiting this evil I would be its next victim, without the slightest doubt. I went to her and lured her into a conversation about the secrets of the caves. I did not tell her about the ancestors' prophetic aphorisms, not merely because I felt sure her community would disdain prophetic wisdom and anything linked to the ancestors but also

because of her instinctive hostility toward these riddles, which
she considered trumped-up superstitions devoid of truth. All the
same, I sang for her, under my breath: "Wherever you come from,
there you'll return, for man, like a caravan, would not be man,
unless he returned to his point of departure." Then, out loud, I
told her about the secrets awaiting her in the caverns and the
other things the ancestors had hidden, treasures that they had
been unable to carry with them into eternity and had been forced
to stash in tombs at the foot of the walls. In my narration, I substituted earthly treasures for the heavenly ones. I recited verses
about the earthly legacy but kept silent about the eternal legacy.
Curiosity flared in her breast, and she followed me like a shadow.
I took her by the heights and scaled the boulders of the southern
cliff faces, chanting to myself the law of arrival and departure
while my tongue kept extolling the vaunted treasures. I followed
twisting trails and cut back and forth between rugged boulders. I
crossed passes, ridges, and peaks that I had reconnoitered during
my explorations in the southern redoubts in the past. I caught
sight of the escape route at last, for I noticed the secret cleft that
had brought me to the labyrinth when I crossed through it one
day, searching for my brethren from the herds' clans.

I slipped through the forbidding cleft, and my shadow slunk
through behind me. I crossed to the other side and traversed in
this stage a distance long enough that our tracks would disappear. Then I turned to toss a question her way: "Are you a jinni
or a person?"

She smiled at me blankly but did not reply. She may have
thought the question senseless. She may have suspected that I
was merely joking. In any case I said, "You arrived at my oasis
borne on the steeds of the jinn, and a demon jinni placed you
in my custody. Is it reasonable that you would be of any lineage
other than the jinn?"

At that she spoke. She spoke while I listened to words like a prophecy issuing from the peak of the mountain rather than from the mouth of a creature named woman: "Master, has there ever been any difference between men and jinn? Didn't you tell me some days ago that you donned the body of a gazelle to save yourself?"

"You're right. The truth is that I shouldn't search for any distinction between men and jinn, between a man and gazelles or Barbary sheep, even between animals and the plants animals consume, or between plants and the earth's soil that nourishes the plants, for I am everything, and everything is really me."

She smiled slyly but said nothing. I too kept my peace, but under my breath I chanted my insane refrain, "Wherever you come from, there you'll return, for man, like a caravan, would not be man unless he returned to his point of departure."

I chanted until I reached the strip of land that is the point of no return. There, at the gap of the unknown, I left her to her fate and fled. Leaping like a Barbary ram, I disappeared behind the boulders that demarcate the deadly opening from the west. I did not pause but continued leaping as though fleeing from my own shadow. I dodged the rocks that obstructed my progress without ever slowing my pace. I did not pause to catch my breath until I had traversed much of the distance on the long way back, while the horizons became covered with the sky's gloom. Then I stretched out to rest. I lay down and dozed off out of sheer exhaustion. I did not awake until the horizons were imbued with daybreak's dazzling firebrand. I jumped up in alarm, for I had witnessed a prophetic vision in my slumber. As I slept, I had seen the she-jinni slither across the earth like a serpent and search in the sun-baked earth for treasure, digging up hard, fiery lumps with both hands. She dug with the insane intensity with which thirsty people excavate parched depths, even though she knew full well she would find nothing there. Despite that certainty, she did not despair. The spirit world mocked her efforts and wrapped them in floods of fraudulent fluids, so that from a distance the poor body seemed a toy teased by the mirage's tongues, which alternately drowned her in the sea and plucked her from its waves, letting her float on the surface of this imaginary flood. This struggle awakened in my heart something I had never experienced before. It awakened in my breast a new inspiration and an insistent whispering that struggled against forgetfulness for a long time before memory told me it was what nations call "compassion." Compassion convulsed me, and I leapt from my sleep and shot off at a gallop over the route I had taken. I raced back with a crazed passion that exceeded that with which I had fled. On my way to the point of no return, I shouted repeatedly, "I never for a moment imagined a child of the jinn could perish of thirst. Forgive me!" I repeated this cry to help me last the distance.

I said aloud, "I'll kill myself if the poor woman has perished before I reach her, because her blood will be on my hands." I wondered about the secret of compassion while I wept. When I finally reached the point of no return, I found I was too late. I heard an uproar there and then saw in the distance the disorganized caravan that had snatched her away before I could reach her.

8 Morning

FINDING MYSELF EMBRACED by solitude once more, I sang my sorrows, chanted my loneliness, and in verse questioned my true nature. I was tormented by yearnings for the unknown and attempted to work off my longings among the rocky boulders. I contrived to cut solid rock into a splendid statue and determined to erect it as a landmark, thus satisfying an unexplained craving that I sensed as a persistent, hushed call in my soul, even though I had never managed to grasp it intellectually. I thought the statue excellent. Washed each morning by rays from my master Ragh, it whispered to the sky a secret it had borrowed from my hands, from my pulse, and from my heart, after this secret had thwarted my tongue. My sole remedy for my weakness was to stroke its torso at dawn each day and shortly after sunset.

After finishing the statue, I felt another strange need. Was it for security? Was it for warmth? Was it for the tranquility that only a nest can provide? I knew the ways of solitude, which likes to wear many veils. I also knew that my thirst for a statue had been an attempt to defend myself against my true love, solitude herself. I had to recognize that the need for a nest was quite simply another face of this beloved, about whom I could swear I was as hard put to live without as to live with. It was a long time before I grasped that this is true of every authentic beloved. I

still do not know whether my need for a nest arose from a desire
for my beloved seclusion or from a desire to avoid her. Certainly
considerations of heat, cold, or wind were not responsible, since
I was accustomed to shielding myself from heat in the shade of
the palm groves and from cold or dust storms in the caves of the
ancestors in the southern mountain range. I had noticed that
this unaccountable need had developed with the passing days
into a bitter hunger, a genuine thirst that would need to be
slaked. I did not feel satisfied again until I had cut from the palm
groves bushy fronds, which I wove into the shape of a cylindri-
cal hut. I thought it was splendid too. I entered it on the sev-
enth day to rest and stretched out in its cavity, which embraced
me as a nest embraces fledglings. It swallowed me the way a
tomb swallows the corpse. I liked this image so much that I
named my cozy nest *azkka*.

Yes, my tomb truly was cozy, and I grew accustomed to sleeping inside it while I roamed far away in visionary dreams. I
sought shelter inside at midday and when evening fell, stretching out on my back and roaming and roaming where there was
no barrier to stop me, no barricade to obstruct my way, no rocks
to scrape my shin, and no rough terrain to impede my progress.
Inside that space, no cares, reptiles, or wild creatures—the offspring of men, jinn, or animals—threatened me. In my nest's
embrace, borne off on one of my trips, I did whatever I wished,
without being visited by any harm or disturbed by any whispered temptations. I would shoot off to the east and west, deeply
furrow the earth, cut the horizons down to size, plunge into the
watery depths, and journey to the sky. I returned once from a
journey to the sky with the question: "Who am I?" It tormented me because I could not answer it. I exhausted myself on these
journeys, thinking I might find the answer in the unfathomable
expanses but returned from each disappointed. Disappointment

left me bitter, dispirited, and melancholy; and I emerged from my cozy redoubt one day to find myself banished once again, exiled from my own land, which I had created with my own hands. I ceased journeying on the wings of dreams and exchanged these voyages through the unknown for voyages of the body. As I wandered aimlessly, I would ask out loud, "Who am I?" and the echo from the mountainous caverns would not vouchsafe any response.

The question "Who am I?" shook my sense of wellbeing, and the whisperings returned, destroying my peace of mind. Then I chased every which way. I did not totally abandon my tomb but did not find inside it the comfort I had discovered there when I first created it. A murky sensation would vibrate my chest and bring me back to the nest once more. The hut's framework continued to taunt me and to fascinate me. My experience is that a fleeting sign always conceals a treasure, which vanishes and is dispersed if we ignore or neglect it. If we strip it bare and wrestle with it, it discloses its secret and gives itself to us. This insight inspired me to resist my murky feeling for a time. In only a matter of weeks its true nature was revealed to me for I saw that I would never feel satisfied or calm or acquire peace of mind unless I married my awe-inspiring stone idol, which I had erected at the foot of the mountain, with the cozy dome, which I had installed in the valley.

I felt that I would put an end to the disruptions, longings, and hunger, if I created a single structure from the two. How could I combine them?

I thought long and hard, and voyaged far and wide in my dreams. When I finished this spiritual investigation, I climbed the mountain and set to work.

I used the noble statue in the foundation and wall for my new dwelling, and it became the house's cornerstone. Wishing to manifest the dream vision through this structure, I told myself that the house could not be a cozy nest unless through its circularity it resembled the sky, the moon, the lord of light Ragh, and the horizon, which arches to encompass the earth. Thus I constructed circular walls like those of the sepulchers of the ancestors. When I finished the walls, I fetched branches, fronds, palm fiber, and palm leaves from my nest below the mountain and wove them over these walls to fashion for this dwelling a domed roof—inspired by the shape of the sky—as an echo of the sky's exaltation.

Once I fulfilled the prophecy, I felt satisfied. Once I felt satisfied, my heart was flooded by ecstasy, longing, and intoxication. So I sang. I sang a touching song of praise for my glorious edifice, to which kinsmen would later bow in prayer, designating it a temple.

Part Three
Grave Talk

Then I reflected on all the works of my hands and on all the toil I had exerted in my labor. In truth, all was vanity and a grasping at the wind, for there is nothing to be gained under the sun.

Ecclesiastes 2: 11

1 Early Morning

I STRUGGLED ALL MY LIFE to reach my eternal father in the higher world, but my father would only consent to appoint me his deputy in the lower world. I wrestled all my days to reach him in the heavens, but he chose to appoint me sovereign of a dirt-covered foothill over which roam the shades that burden the earth.

In later times, caravans stormed me. I did not know whether they were commanded by jinn from the spirit world or by the spawn of men. I asked them repeatedly what they really were, but every time they replied, in a tone suggesting veiled condescension, "The fact is that we are none but you." I also interrogated the nobles about the circumstances that had cast them into my home-place, which was protected by the desert's wiles. They would smile furtively and respond that cunning prophets had guided them. If I chanced to ask their destination, they would answer ungrammatically, "From where we come, to there returning we go." Some were mirthful and others painfully stern, but I saw their uniform enthusiasm for late parties at which people sang. They enjoyed spending their evenings with me while recuperating from the terrors of the route and would converse with each other in their pidgin tongue as if exchanging verses of poetry. Occasionally they sang sad laments or launched into long conversations about riddles like hope, heroism, and happiness. At times they continued their chatter till dawn. Before they set off again, they would leave me various types of meat and tools, along with other gifts, in exchange for the water. One of them happened to leave me a present that was responsible for robbing me of my peace of mind and turning the oasis upside down. The gift was some vile dust that danced in the rays of light. The man said it was called gold dust. The leader of the caravan told me that this dust could be exchanged for commodities but could also harm people, change enemies into bosom buddies, buy protection, bolster civilization and destroy cities, transform the lowest to the highest and the highest to the lowest, subjugate the spirit, enslave other people, overcome any redoubt, and work any miracle. He finished by saying that it was a rebellious demon, notwithstanding its gaiety, and could turn into an evil thing, unless its owner handled it wisely. I thirstily imbibed his account. I did not, however, have occasion to use the dust until much later—when the seduction of taxation distracted me from the truth about it—for I bartered my water for the various types of commodities that leaders had devised throughout the desert: food, clothing, livestock, and even other human beings.

Yes, water brought me slaves, vassals, and women of the type known as slave girls. I would cleave to their bodies when I felt a need for warmth, for I discovered by fondling them that their companionship served as an antidote for loneliness. I also modeled on their conceits some amulets that were useful as a balm to heal the body's ills, even though the conduct of these women and the fluctuation of their humors often agitated me to such a degree that I was reminded of my first she-jinni. I could, now that I was migrating between the embraces of women I owned, diagnose her as having been afflicted by what the sages of migratory tribes call "melancholy."

The symptoms of this disease I found in the behavior of another seductively beautiful female jinni who arrived at the oasis with a prodigious cortège. She enchanted me with her voice, and I fell in love with her. It seems the gift of song was the secret snare by which this new she-jinni captivated me, not her beauty, since the voice, in its true nature, is profound, whereas beauty by itself, as experience has taught me, is a shell. I am now willing to acknowledge myself a coward, for my attempts to free myself from her were not inspired by her eccentricities but by my fear of loving her. I had cohabited with solitude for such a long time that solitude had become my true love and I was afraid of cheating on her with another playmate. Despite my secret conviction that this was the case, even so, I tried to outwit my certainty and to convince myself that my rejection of the beautiful woman's passionate love was caused by my eagerness for calm and peace of mind. I used this contrived lie with the questioning men who crowded round me the day I ordered her expelled from the oasis. They obeyed, expelling her one morning as I had commanded, but I was flabbergasted when everyone in the oasis trailed after her. I could not believe it. At first I suspected that the throngs had followed merely to satisfy their curiosity or that they had turned out to bid her farewell as they did for important people. What really affected me, however, was their songs, which were genuine, heart-rending laments. So I dashed after them only to discover that the cause of the tumult was the beautiful woman's singing. Yes, the she-jinni was raising her voice in a sorrowful song that affected me so deeply I was unable to walk. I halted halfway to them, weeping. My suppressed longing was roused, and I wept some more. Then I stopped my ears with my index fingers to stifle the sound so I could walk again.

With the sound stilled and the impediment of my feet lifted, I set off at a gallop. I rushed up to the weeping throngs. I caught sight of the vassals, who were clustered around her, lamenting and crying. I yelled as loudly as I could, "Bring her back! Bring her back! Bring her back!"

They brought her back, but I did not return. I obtained the lady of song for my home and as part of the exchange lost the lord of stillness. I kept to myself while I pondered my confusion. I did not conclude this self-examination until the spirit world whispered to me another truth, saying that a man passionately in love with solitude will never feel at peace with those passionately in love with women. I discounted this insight and surrendered to her, hoping to be able to forget. She attempted to compound from her embraces an antidote for my malady. She sang sorrowful songs to me in our bedchamber until I swooned. She did everything she could to grant me happiness, an enigma as mysterious as the desert. How preposterous! I perceived that happiness is a talisman that rightfully belongs to others, to people whose knowledge, pursuits, and travels are limited. Devotees of solitude are destined to take solace in silence, because their mission is to keep company with the spirit world. My heart was flooded by longing. I felt stifled and fled to the caves of the ancestors in the southern peaks. There I examined the wisdom that the first peoples had etched on the cavern walls. I argued at length with the spirit world and did not return from my fugue until I had received prophetic guidance. I entered the oasis one night and sequestered myself with the wisest and most trustworthy of my vassals to share the substance of this revelation with him. I could see disapproval in his eyes, but he obeyed. He undertook to bring me what I needed the following day: a leather bag of a depressing color, filled with an even more depressing powder. I hid this in my pocket and waited until the servants brought the food. Then I tossed all the powder into the broth. The she-jinni came, consumed the broth, and then ate. She sang until midnight, even though she had put enough poison into her belly to annihilate an entire caravan.

I awoke expecting to find her corpse, but she disappointed me. I ordered my chief vassal to appear so I could inquire about the effects of the poison. The man said the effects were slow and that I should be patient. After a day and a night she felt nauseous, complained of feeling dizzy, and lay down to nurse herself. I assumed that the hour of release was at hand and wept sorrowful tears, mixed with tears of joy. I was sad because I did not know how I would confront the void she would leave in my life when I lost her. I was as joyful as a child, because I would finally be liberated once my doll had been smashed. Even so, neither my sorrow nor my joy lasted long, because the servant whom I had stationed by her bedside as a spy under the pretense of caring for her informed me the next morning that she had indeed suffered from the pains of fever at first and that she had sweated profusely and combated demons in a nightmare but had sneezed three times after midnight and each time had expelled from her nostrils sinister, evil-colored snot. The dolt added that he believed these discharges of mucous had freed her from her ailment and cured her. I listened dumbfounded to his chatter. Then I found myself repeating, "She-jinni! She-jinni! The lord of lords is a she-jinni." I went to investigate in person. She gave me a look in which I saw everything. I could see that she knew, and forgave me, but wondered why. In fact, in no time at all, she asked, "Why?"

I pretended not to understand, but she gazed into my eyes with the look of one who knows everything. So I confessed, "I wouldn't have done it if I wasn't in love with you. You know that better than anyone."

"Is the beloved destined to die by the lover's hand?"

"Yes, indeed!"

"By what law?"

"By the law of fear."

"To which fear do you refer?"

"The fear of confusion."

"Confusion?"

"No, the fear of anxiety."

"What foul talk!" she exclaimed.

"I don't understand," I said.

"Don't you know that love is the only treasure we don't forfeit even if we reward it with a calamity?"

"I know that love is a treasure. I know that love is the most precious treasure, but solitude inevitably risks death to defend herself, because she too is love, love of a unique variety."

"Rubbish!"

"Are you a jinni?" I asked.

"Are you human?" she countered.

"Yes, indeed."

"You're lying!"

"I don't understand."

"I meant to say that in the heart of each person is a creature spawned by the jinn and that in the body of each jinni is a creature spawned by men."

"Who are you?" I asked.

"I'm from a country where there is no distinction between men and jinn."

"Is it the country of longing?"

"You're right. It is the country of longing, from which you also came, before you went into exile."

"I will devote three out of every four of my days to my lady if you tell me the truth about the country of longing I knew before I entered forgetfulness."

"I don't want your days in payment for the deal. Give me your heart."

"For the sake of knowledge I will not withhold even my heart."

"I know you yearn to hear news of your fatherland, since you desire a father."

"Have you been granted news of the father too?"

"Nothing is hidden from a messenger."

"A messenger?"

"A messenger of destiny, I come to your lands from the distant country of Asaho to share your kingdom and bedchamber and to sing the glories of the eternal father."

"Bravo! Bravo!"

"I will bear you offspring that will perpetuate the clan of the original homeland to leave a trace and to fulfill a pledge I have made."

Then she raised her voice in a song of longing that made me forget who I was. When I regained my senses, I heard her complete the prophecy: "From today forward, your offspring will be the progeny of Targa, and tongues will constantly speak of them, because they are, of all the clans, a clan with a secret. Their true name will remain a talisman among people, as the law decreed. All the same, they are a wretched clan, for their destiny is exile. So, beware!"

2   Midday

AT FIRST I SHARED my bedroom with Tin Hinan, because I considered this cunning creature my spouse. Once the people made me priest of the temple, the goddess Tanit visited me, while I was between sleeping and waking, and asked me to bring my spouse into the shrine to keep me company there too. I did that, although I obeyed out of respect for the gods' secrets and not out of any conviction about the true nature of women. All the same, I soon discovered the wisdom of this advice. In fact the she-jinni's voice, which had once shaken the people's souls, was now able to awaken a similar response in the souls of the gods. From the first day she sang of eternal longing inside my old temple, which I had constructed on the mountainside as a home for myself, the world has not ceased to resound with her heavenly hymn. It was the first psalm heard by the walls of a desert temple. Apparently the supplication pleased the heavens, for the lords of the spirit world courted her and selected her from among all the people to bear the burden of prophecy. Thus her dreams became revelations that were never tardy or false. Some scholars say that Targa's emblem, which the engineers placed on the corners of the walls to serve as a symbol for that magnificent oasis, was actually a revelation from the principal goddess Tanit, who confided it to her beloved temple priestess Tin Hinan, who in turn revealed it to the earth's master builders. My vassals told me that there was a symbolic meaning to the triangular emblem. The first angle represented virility and the second femininity. The reference of the third angle had been lost, but the quest for it excited a lengthy debate during the course of which some people pointed out its supremacy and discussed its power, even though it was shielded and concealed from sight. At the same time, another team attributed the lost reference in the figure to reality itself, for reality is nothing more or less than a sign. The third faction was more daring and made it quite clear they believed that the third corner of the emblem represented the goddess Tanit, because she had decreed that the body of the earth would not stand upright unless there was within it some aspect of her character. Evidence was provided by the extraordinary care the engineers took in designing the emblem and in drawing it on every structure, for it became a symbol of the entire desert tribe. They first placed it on my old house, which they insisted on using as a temple for the religion of longing when they summoned me to be a priest for the shrine. They used my yearning for my father to justify their request with the same enthusiasm with which they summoned Tin Hinan to join me and become the priestess, citing her passion for songs of longing. This was even before I revealed to people the desert goddess' advice, which she gave me during a visit when I was between sleep and wakefulness.

The day they decided to fetter me with political leadership as well as the priesthood I was terrified by the burden, but they flocked to me and told me in unison, "We have selected you to govern us, because we would be wrong to trust a man who has not suffered. For similar reasons, we have chosen you to serve as guardian over our temple, because we are certain that our worldly affairs will not prosper unless someone with access to dream visions takes charge. There is nothing to be gained from a ruler who does not unite pain and prophecy in his heart."

Astonished by the clarity of their insight, I asked, "Who are you?"

They replied in the ancient language of riddles, "We are a community which prefers to speak of the shadow when referring to the shadow's original and which gestures toward the shadow when speaking of the original." This made me sure that they were a group of that small band that roams the desert and that some call "Kel Iba," which in Tuareg means "people of the spirit" or "spirits." Others refer to them as "people of the spirit world." Then the vassals went all out in construction projects, drawing on the assistance of the throngs of people who by that time had gathered in the oasis. The first project they put in place was the incorporation of my old house, which had been turned into a temple on the advice of their priests, into my new house. The sanctuary occupied the place of the heart in the structure. They named the central part, which was crowned with the emblem of the goddess, "House of the Spirit," because of the way it was conjoined with the newer house, which they called the "Sublime Gate," because it rested on the flank of a knoll overlooking the growing oasis.

The sages were not satisfied, however. They gazed at the sky, admiring its handsome light. They searched everywhere and excavated the earth, working tirelessly to extract a mineral the color of light. This they named "lime." They set right to work using it to whitewash the walls of the temple, turning it white, since they judged the color of daylight auspicious and wished to show respect for Ragh's immortal gift. After that, they came to me and wrested me from my seclusion in the cave of the ancestors. They were singing charms of longing as sacred chants. They took me by the hand and led me to the lofty edifice, which the white stucco rendered even more majestic, imposing, and grand. There they surprised me with melancholy songs and caught me off-guard. Three of the fiercest of the team of sages pounced on me. One wrapped his arms around me. A second man fit a leather mask over my face, and the third chanted the charm in my ear: "You are the scion of the lord of lords, Ragh, who deserted you one day, for he only deserts the creature he loves. Thus you became, from that day forward, eternally, Anubi. Had it not been for your exile, we would never have appointed you sovereign of the lower world and we would not have dared to make you deputy, or caliph, over the earth for the lord of lords." So the mask of Anubi, following this secret ceremony, became an amulet I used to conceal my face whenever I entered the temple, either to be alone, to ponder a concern of mine or of the people's, or to beseech the spirit world to inspire me with a prophecy.

After these sages finished the house of the spirit, it was the turn of the house of worldly affairs, which they called the "Sublime House." After examining the heavens again they returned from those vast expanses with a new prophetic mission. They accosted me inside my house this time, shackled me, and jerked me back and forth. When they stopped that, I assumed my bout of punishment was concluded, but they grasped whips and flogged me. They whipped me until I started bleeding. Then they left me in a corner while they chanted charms that meant nothing to me. Once they had finished, their attention turned back to me. They crowned my head with a blue, leather turban imprinted with the goddess Tanit's triangle and handed me the hilt of a wooden staff, which was topped by another emblem of the goddess: two intersecting, straight lines. Next they belted into my ear a musical incantation, as if they were singing: "We caused you pain, even though you weren't guilty, to give you a taste of how tyranny feels to an innocent person. We have crowned you with this blue headgear so that you will know that

the scion of the heavens came from the heavens and will return
to the heavens. Thus his status here below is temporary. We have
placed the staff in your right hand for you to use in greeting, not
in killing. You should realize that we have not appointed you to
rule over the living but over dead people who think they're alive.
You should set forth, because from today on, you are a shadow
charged with care of the shadows that burden the earth." Then I
heard them sing in unison about longing, using the tune "Saho,"
which speaks of the exile of the clan in ancient days. I detected
the melodious voice of Tin Hinan.

After this melodic initiation rite the master builders decided
to make architectural history in the oasis. They circulated
another enigmatic saying, referring to a building as a song in
space and to a tune as a structure in time. Next they debated at
length the dawn of being, first discussing its relationship with
the spirit world. Then they turned their attention to visible
bodies, beginning with the sky and culminating with the arc of
the horizon, which encircles the desert. They discussed in their
recondite language the puzzle of perfection, saying that a talisman will inevitably be circular, because worship of the divine,
like the circle, has no beginning or end. They decided to shelter themselves inside buildings inspired by worship and began
erecting rounded corners while chanting sorrowful songs that
portrayed a building's essence as a melody in space and a melody
as a structure situated in time. These presumptuous fellows did
not stop until they had arranged rows of circular houses into a
necklace around the oasis, thus creating a perimeter wall that
bristled with platoons of the goddess' triangular emblem. They
left the buildings earth-colored for a time, but soon the sages
argued among themselves and raised their voices in debate
before reaching a consensus about the essence of color. It is
reported that they said that white is the color associated with

nobles, since it is the only color that borrows its sanctity from Ragh's expression, which everyone sees in the color of daylight. So they gave a free hand to the vassals and engineers, who spread the walls of the houses with the whitest types of lime, excavated from neighboring valley bottoms.

Natural protective boundaries of sand and rock notwithstanding, people contrived to reach the oasis. Clans from the four corners of the desert mixed in suspect settlements where people tracing their lineage back to the people of the spirit world rubbed shoulders with other communities that traced their roots back to distant nations of unknown identity. They lived harmoniously in that valley and intermarried. Then the sages decided to advance another step toward the realization of their dream. They began to build with stone and to erect ever larger buildings, relying on a team of magicians allegedly from the east. They were said to excel in parleying with the spirit world, in mastering stone, and in solving the talismanic riddles of the earth. These fellows assisted the sages in erecting walls. Their engineering was inspired by the circularity of the temple, which was slipped into the heart of the palace. I heard these wretches sing, while they labored industriously, tunes that I admit awakened in my heart a forgotten sorrow, possibly because they referred to the riddle of creation:

> We who love stone
> Are the people of prophetic counsel,
> The sages,
> The shapers of existence.
> We have created the world.

I appropriated this song from these people and repeated it to myself in my hideaway, even though its lyrics' arrogance and braggadocio made me nervous. So I was not astonished when a team of these scoundrels from the east used furnaces to smelt metals and to produce a lethal material they named "iron." It was judged by the better people to be inimical to the sovereignty of the spirit world. All the same, that faction's insatiable appetite for research was far from satisfied. The vassals told me that they had met with the sages before emerging from their conference with another prophetic directive to process the metal and to mint from it a disk they named "coin." These coins they dropped into people's hands to serve as markers for commercial exchanges between caravan leaders. Base metal coins predominated for a time, but soon they replaced these with gold dust, which they smelted, poured into molds, and then minted into coins as well.

I had not grasped the truth of the prophetic counsel of the wanderer who had once given me gold dust in lieu of merchandise and who had told me about gold's exceptional characteristics, until I saw what the team from the east did with it. They decreed, after consulting the sages as usual, that one should covet it and attempt to procure it by any means whatsoever. They were the first to broadcast this propaganda, which spread like a plague through the nations. It stated that gold dust is a sacred gift, not a terrestrial metal. That this metal's traits mimic those of the lord of lords was cited as evidence for their claim. It was said that gold dust was related to Ragh both in appearance and in substance; in appearance because of its color and in substance because of its immortality. On account of this despicable claim, many people became even more passionately enamored of it than of the lord of lords, and competed with each other to acquire it. Although this hoarding of gold succeeded in saving the oasis from famines many times, that despicable powder introduced to the oasis major crimes unknown before.

Worship of the metal became widespread, and many people erred for the first time. They erred, because they conspired, plotted, plundered, and thus abandoned the spirit world. Not surprisingly, the matter ended with one native son raising his hand to slay his brother and then seizing the other's share of this ignoble metal. The first crime the oasis experienced was committed with a weapon forged from iron and concerned a gold bar. Then I remembered the counsel of the wanderer and felt certain that his words had not been simply an admonition but a prophecy and that the wanderer had not been simply a passerby but a prophet in the rags of a vagabond.

3 Afternoon

I WAS PROWLING through the caves of the ancestors in the southern mountain range when my slave Hur arrived, bearing good news.

I descended the mountain behind him and heard the hymns of longing before I reached the base of the cliff. Circumambulating the sanctuary were sages preceded by the oldest and most venerable one. He carried a doll, which was wrapped in a hide lined with goat hair, tossed it in the air from time to time, and then caught it again as he raised his voice in a sacred, heart-rending psalm to conciliate the spirit world. The group of apparitions scurrying behind him quickly snatched the tune from his lips and repeated it after him in a melancholy harmony of a sweetness known to tribes only in songs of the people of the spirit world. I attempted to make out the words of the psalm, even though I had failed repeatedly on previous occasions. I failed this time as well. Therefore I assumed that this clan did not use a desert tongue in its songs and was gibbering in the language of the people of the spirit world. Once when I asked one of these sages the secret meaning carried by these songs, he responded with a murky question: "Would hymns be hymns if they were rendered in an earthly tongue?" So I swallowed my curiosity and never asked about their meaning again. Here they were now, swaying, reeling, and chanting incomprehensible gibberish. I must confess that the sweetness of this gibberish is beyond compare and far exceeds that of any language.

I walked ever closer to this congregation and heard for the first times an infant's cries, which reached my ears faintly—as if rising from the depths of a well—and melodiously, as if mimicking the sages' hymn to mock them. I stopped to ask myself, "Is it conceivable that this doll they're tossing in the air is my child?" The conjecture shook me, but I gained control of myself and stepped forward.

Then one of them rushed toward me, took me aside, and said, "This isn't done. This isn't done." When I attempted to free myself so I could reach the people, he stubbornly prevented me, saying, "We mustn't allow emotion to infringe on our law in any way." Seeing the determined look in my eye, he gestured to one of the group's demons. He arrived in the wink of an eye to assist the sly dog. He too blocked my way. The cunning sage said apologetically, "We're not celebrating the birth of a child. We're singing to celebrate the birth of the prophecy." I did not understand. I did not comprehend his riddle but did not ask for any clarification.

He must have detected my silent incomprehension, for he explained, "Today the desert witnesses the birth of the desert. Today creation witnesses the birth of the race that the spirit world wishes to serve as the secret heart of nations." I remembered a prophetic saying of Tin Hinan and stole a glance to see what the insolent fellows were doing to my child. I saw the swarms of people enter the temple. As I listened intently, the solemn hymn swelled to swallow the newborn's sobs. I tried to trail after them, but the two sages restrained me once more. The first said, "Not before the spirit world grants permission."

I was about to ask, "But when will that happen?"

The wily strategist again read my mind, because I heard him say as enigmatically as ever, "Today is not like other days. Today the desert witnesses a birth. You must relax, be patient, and wait." I waited a long time, for the rites of birth were not concluded until after midnight, when their elder came to tell me that the congregation had only just then finished praying. When I inquired about the prayer ritual, he ignored my question and burst into an account of the purification. He said that the infant's spirit had been cleansed with a flash from the light of Ragh and that his body had been bathed in spring water, because the spirit is the offspring of light, whereas the body is born of water and clay. Then he chanted an incantation set to music before adding that the congregation had unanimously adopted the name Ara for the infant as a hopeful augury for the future, yielding to the wishes of prophecy. I was upset by this choice but suppressed my anger, for I had decided to give him a different name—Hur— chosen for me by another prophecy. I would take the name of my loyal slave for my good omen and try in this way to deceive the female ghouls that watch for any chance to pounce on the nobles' sons to abduct and swap for changelings descended from the jinn or from the tribes of the spirit world. I certainly did not know it at the time, but in this fashion I was, unconsciously, countering the prophecy of the female soothsayer who informed me one day that the offspring of slaves would take control of my kingdom and arrogate to themselves my offspring's due, leaving me to return empty-handed from my journey. I immediately ascribed to my son the name of my slave, hoping this name would protect him against exile. I could not learn until later that this would be his destiny. The termination of the oasis' celebration of the birth, however, was followed by a confession. I had scarcely stretched out one night when Tin Hinan burst in upon my solitude to tell me a secret. She said that she was not a foreigner and that she had never belonged to the nations of migrants. Rather she was blood kin, and not just related to me but that very sister whom I had once known and who had frequently sheltered me in her embrace. I did not say a word. I stared at her incredulously for a time.

She smiled mischievously and nodded her head "yes" when I shouted, "The priest's daughter?" I was shocked and voiced my astonishment. She explained that she had deliberately disguised herself in foreign garb to fulfill a prophetic dictum. I was silent. She did not wish to complete her confession. So I quizzed her to learn the import of this dictum.

During a painful silence that lasted a long time, she said nothing. Finally she said, "I did that to safeguard our progeny."

When I gave her a questioning look, she explained, "You know fathers are figments of the imagination."

"What?"

"You know better than anyone else how spurious fatherhood is."

"Fatherhood spurious?"

"You've wasted your life chasing after your father and have reaped nothing but the wind."

"But you told me once that my father was your father, the priest, whom I killed to avenge my mother."

"You killed your father's shadow. You didn't kill your father."

"What are you saying?"

"You were right to want to kill him; fathers must die, since a father is always a shadow. A father is always a specter. The father we know is not a father. The true father is an unknown apparition. Should he decide to renounce his concealment and to descend on us, bringing us glad tidings of his paternity, we must resort to force and do away with him with our own hands, since he is our father's shadow and not our father. He is a spurious father, not the legitimate one."

"A wanderer told me a riddle like this once, but I didn't believe it."

"Back then, you killed the shadow of our father, but our father slipped away again. The mother's status, on the other hand, is different."

"Tell me about the mother."

"If the father is spurious, the mother is always authentic."

"Bravo!"

"A mother we don't know is not a mother. The father we do know isn't a father."

"Riddles certainly fascinate you, desert nation."

"Be a child and you'll see that what the daughter of the desert has said is anything but a riddle. Return to the cradle of a new-born and you'll know that the mother who plucked you from her belly, in whose arms you were carried, and in whose embrace you slept, is the only true one and that anyone else is fraudulent and counterfeit."

"Fortunately for you, I can revert to my childhood. Fortunately for you, I had a greater sense of my mother's presence than any other child and a greater sense of my father's absence. Had I not lost my father I would not have begun my journey through the labyrinth and would not have lost my talisman while wandering."

"I've come in disguise to you to help care for the talisman."

"Is this another riddle?"

"Not so fast! I've come to bear you, from my womb, offspring who will trace their lineage to your mother's clan, for you have not produced them from the womb of a foreigner but from the blood of a woman who is your sister. This is the only amulet that can safeguard the offspring of the desert against extinction."

"But what about the father?"

"Haven't we agreed on the fraudulent nature of the father? In this game, you are only a passing specter. Be careful, for the only refuge you'll ever find for your offspring is my embrace."

"Do you suppose this will quench my thirst? Do you think that rescuing my offspring will make up for my failure to find my father?"

"Leave your progeny to me and search for your father to your heart's content, even though I'm certain you have sprung from a fraud and are becoming one yourself."

"But what status will be granted me by the law of descent concerning the mother's descendants?"

"It suffices that it will protect them from a she-demon named loss."

"Loss is truly a she-demon. Loss is a ghoul that threatens the entire desert nation."

"One must cling firmly to the mother's tent peg to preserve the riddle of life over the course of a life. One must fasten the rope tight to the woman's tent peg, because woman is the mistress of this world. Man cannot be relied on, because he, in the game, is always a disappearing dream. If man weren't so obtuse, you wouldn't have wasted your life searching for your father, miserable spouse."

I perceived that she had deprived me of my strongest arguments, not because I had missed my father or killed my father or my father's shadow, as the priestess referred to him and as the wanderer referred to all fathers, but because I had always lost my way to my father and had found myself isolated, forsaken, and lost whenever I thought I had grasped the reins of my truth. Thus I was content to accept the curse of Anubi as my destiny. Without meaning to, I stammered, "Anubi's fate was atrocious. Let my clan trace their lineage according to the mother's law, or any law, so long as that saves them from the fate of Anubi."

Then I heard the priestess prophesy: "From this day forward, the banner will be in the hand of the sister's son and not in the hand of the father's son."

With this, however, the priestess did not just place the staff of sovereignty in the hand of the sister's offspring but also laid the foundation stone for the law authorizing marriage with one's sister.

4   Sunset

ONE DAY, SHORTLY AFTER SUNSET, the sages escorted me to the congregation and their leaders told me that the time had come for me to assume power. They first discussed the law, telling me that its prophetic dicta are divided into two parts. The first half facilitates the affairs of this world and the second preserves our relationship with the spirit world. To the second belong those abstruse texts devoted to the community's incontrovertible class structure. The most venerable of them stepped toward me and thrust in my face a scrap of hide imprinted with cryptic symbols. Then he said that the tribe was to be divided, according to the mandate of the spirit world, into three authentic castes. The offspring of Ragh would constitute the head, the progeny of the goddess Yeth, the spine and torso, and the clan of Seth, the flexible limbs. Then he examined the talismanic writing on the scrap of leather for some time before adding that the spirit world's wisdom decreed the first clan should assume responsibility for governance, following matrilineal descent, on condition that they owned nothing and they kept their hands off worldly vanities, taking their cue from the divine progenitor, who possesses nothing, since he is sovereign over all.

Then he spoke of the second clan's mission, saying that they were the cavalry of the supreme goddess and sons of the mother who gave birth to everything. They were destined to enjoy

material possessions and to appoint kings from among the
descendants of Ragh, on condition that they themselves never
attempted to rule.

The strategic clan's mission was to be cunning and to investigate everything, no matter how obvious or obscure, searching
out whatever was useful, without defying the talisman.

Then this wily sage fell silent. He remained silent for such a
long time that this stillness swallowed the world. When he
returned from his spiritual journey, he proclaimed the final piece
of the prophecy: "There will be disturbances and the whole tribe
will be destroyed the day the law is violated, whether the lineage of Ragh covets possession of worldly vanities, the lineage of
Yeth wishes to seize power, or the carnal self seduces the lineage
of Seth to exceed the boundaries of what is appropriate in their
pursuit of knowledge." He fell silent, and stillness reigned over
the earth once more. Then he concluded his pronouncement by
saying, "Thus ends the revelation!" He approached me and
handed me the pieces of hide imprinted with talismans. He
bowed to me so deferentially that I was shaken. In a grave tone
he recited, "You, master, from today forward, are master of these
texts. You, master, from today forward are sovereign over the
desert." Then he gestured to the row of sages, who approached
me, one at a time.

They bowed to my transient body, repeating the prophetic
saying as if chanting a supplication raised to the spirit world:
"You, master, from today forward, are master of these texts. You,
master, from today forward, are sovereign over the desert." Then
the senior sage continued his address, emphasizing the need to
respect the three goals. He said that a truth that cannot rest on
one goal must inevitably rest on three but emended this statement to caution against the fourth goal, affirming that concealed truth contradicts surface truth, which is demolished if

the fourth goal is lost. After that I heard him raise his voice in a heart-rending hymn of longing. Its sweetness set my heart to dancing and stirred tears from my eye, so I wept involuntarily. Still singing, he stepped toward me. Then he whispered in poetic words: "Master, man is a prophetic saying. The division is real. Don't forget it!" Then . . . then he withdrew. He did not merely withdraw; he vanished like a mirage one pursues. He vanished and with him vanished the rows of sages. I never saw them again after that.

The sages left me to my own devices. As emptiness settled into my heart, I felt the void. I returned alone, feeling isolated and abandoned, despite the existence of throngs of people in the oasis and despite the presence of my consort beside me. That day I realized that there are creatures whose true nature is veiled from us until we lose them. I also realized that there are creatures no woman can replace, even if by virtue of her wisdom she is a priestess, and for whose absence even throngs of the very best sort of men are no consolation. I realized that loneliness is a beast that cannot be tamed, even by someone we choose for that task. It is, rather, a secret frittered away by people we do not attempt to befriend and do not seek out. I was obliged, once more, to recognize that I was none other than Anubi and that the destiny of Anubi in this desert is solitude.

Even so, I remembered the prophetic counsel of the venerable master who granted me custody of the hide texts and who appointed me ruler over the desert. Thus I was forced to come to terms with my destiny and to take charge of things myself this time. The fact is that my motive in assuming power was not a sense of obligation but as a way of dispelling my loneliness and annihilating my ennui. Why shouldn't I have some fun?

I observed what was around me. I observed what was inside me. I saw that this game required rules. So I decided to begin by selecting for my sessions an entourage to console me for the loss of the college of sages. I was obliged to search the leather texts to find support for this in the prophetic aphorisms entrusted to me by the sages. Relying on these, I saw the importance of doing things in threes. I went to the cave of the ancestors in the southern cliff face and sequestered myself there for a time before returning to my oasis with a vision. I seated my consort beside me and ordered the vassals to bring me the nobles of the tribes. I told them that the Law in its dicta had praised the Trinitarian approach and that I proposed to select from each community a man who would not begrudge me his advice, should I request his counsel, and who would serve as my companion in my daily life, should stifling loneliness afflict me. They murmured their approval. I wasted no time in surrounding myself with this group and then immediately asked them, "Will the lords of the people confirm that we will not be blamed for having fun?"

They were quick to protest in unison, "Of course not, master. Absolutely not!"

"I shall shower my wealth on anyone who can show me how to dispel worry from our world except through entertainment."

The group straightaway shouted to one another, "The sages of our tribes buried their heads in prophecies till their eyesight blurred and discovered no other truth in this world than entertainment."

"But you, lords of the people, know better than the other folk the maxim that in our world the law governs everything, including entertainment."

"Of course, our master: entertainment too is governed by the will of the law."

"The era of the lords of the law has passed, and a void hangs over our oasis. Their reality, however, did not reside in their bodies, which have passed away, but in their wise sayings, which they have bequeathed to us."

At this point a voice brazenly raised a question that I thought reeked of veiled insolence: "Does it make sense, my master, to claim the sages advocated jesting?"

The man beside him, however, saved me the trouble of rebutting him, for he said, "We will perish, master, of boredom, if we don't rule in favor of entertainment. A child must be an infant to lack the ability to play. My goat gave birth to a melancholy kid that acted weird. He wouldn't frolic with the other kids or respond to his mother's nudges. He spent the whole day staring into space and stayed up all night examining the stars. I saw a sorrow in his eyes I could compare only to that in the eyes of wanderers, exiles, and sages. I was sure some jinni's spawn was dwelling in this kid's body. It appears I guessed right, because the sorrowful look in this wretch's eyes increased to a point that augured ill. Do you know what happened next? One day I saw him climb a boulder on the cliff face and then cast himself into the abyss. He perished, my master, just as any creature that loses the ability to have fun perishes."

A murmur spread through the assembly. One man shouted, "Your kid was a man, not a beast or a jinni!"

I gestured for them to be still, and they hushed. I studied a piece of text in my lap before observing, "The sages advocated a threefold approach. To reinforce the footers of the sacred building, there must be three pillars."

This metaphorical reference was too abstruse for the crowd, and people looked apprehensive. I tried to elucidate the allusion: "Our master Ragh is overhead, on earth there are creatures, and in the souls of the people there is wisdom." I concluded, "The fourth pillar of the building, however, is a blunder. Beware!"

Voices repeated after me, "The fourth pillar is a blunder."

"In wombs, the sperm is restless and the fetuses develop, waiting for the hour of birth, which no one knows for certain. All the same, I have thought that waiting will slay us with loneliness. This is why I thought I would choose from each of your tribes a man who would take a place beside me in the council to act as the nucleus of the future clan, until the sperm develops out of sight and the embryos are delivered from the wombs."

They repeated with all the intoxication of singers touched by ecstatic longing, "Until the sperm develops out of sight and the embryos are delivered from the wombs."

"But don't get so carried away that you forget the whole thing is in jest."

"The whole thing is in jest."

"I don't want you to neglect your carnal self or to err by arrogating to yourselves the role of the secret being waiting in the womb. Act, rather, with an understanding that you divert yourselves in order to forget."

At that point, one of the nobles approached and whispered to me, as if confiding a secret, "But what is it, my master, that you want us to forget by jesting?"

The wretch infuriated me with his question, but I enjoyed my response to him: "You'll kill yourselves, if you don't forget you're alive. You'll share the fate of the kid that your companion described, if you don't amuse yourselves."

Anxiety reigned once again, so I chanted this appeal: "The text from the spirit world, O people of Targa, says that the offspring of Ragh will be the tribe's head. So, have you chosen for me from among yourselves a child of Ragh to be his deputy on earth?"

Silence was universal. People exchanged surreptitious glances, nudged each other, and whispered to one another.

Their consultation produced this response, "Do we dare, our master, select a creature to be Ragh's vice-regent on earth when our assembly is headed by the descendant of Ragh chosen by the spirit world to be Ragh's authentic deputy, not his counterfeit deputy?"

"I am grateful for your confidence but fear that for me to remain with you will constitute an abuse of the texts and an infraction of the law of entertainment."

The lady of my house and priestess of the temple cast me a disapproving look. Apparently one of the men seated nearby saw that look, for he took the offensive: "Doesn't our master fear the spirit world will be provoked by his reluctance to assume the sovereignty that was his destiny from the start?"

"Will it harm this sovereignty if the nation goes a bit overboard in combating alienation through their jests?"

"I once heard a clever man predict a grievous end, master, for nations that dare to mix earnestness with jest."

"If you can tell me the truth about earnestness, I'll give you half my kingdom. If you can tell me the truth about jesting, I'll give you the other half."

At this point the lady seated beside me intervened for the first time: "We do not control our destinies; our destinies control us. We may wager what our hands possess but have no right to wager what possesses us. Our master may throw into play everything he possesses. Our master, however, has no right to throw into play the hand that controls him."

"To what hand do you refer, mistress?"

"The hand of destiny, the hand that threw you into the arena of this oasis, placing it before you, the hand that installed you not only as head of Targa but also as its guardian."

"But what can a sovereign do when his breast is mangled by melancholy and his heart tempted by wandering?"

She ignored my question, however, and delivered another prophecy to the assembly: "Sovereignty, our master, is what holds sway over us. We aren't sovereign over sovereignty."

"Doesn't the sovereign have the right to free himself from his power?"

"Certainly not!"

"In our lady's law, is sovereignty a curse?"

"Sovereignty for the sovereign is a destiny, not a curse. Do you know who you are?"

"I? I, lady, am a wanderer."

"Certainly not! You were a wanderer, master, before the fates shackled you with the oasis. You were a wanderer, master, before the spirit world fettered you with sovereignty. From today forward, you have no name besides sovereign, no homeland besides sovereignty, and no god besides sovereignty. You are the monarchy, and the monarchy is you. How can you abdicate a kingship the spirit world has granted you as a sacred trust without also abdicating your true nature? How can you renounce this trust without renouncing your self?"

"With what antidote, then, is the master of melancholy to be healed? By what antidote, then is the victim of longing to be cured?"

I did not hear her response. I did not hear it, because ecstasy had flooded my heart and longing had overflowed my spirit. The unidentified tune became ever louder in my ears. I was choked by a tear and found that my body was swaying to the right and left, in time with the beat. My tongue picked up the refrain right away. This was an anxious song that affected my muscles the way a prophecy affects the heart. I sang, and everyone sang with me, although the priestess declined the invitation. She stared at me with veiled curiosity. When I stopped to catch my breath, she leaned toward me to say, "Don't be foolhardy."

I did not know what she meant and began singing again. I sang and everyone resumed singing with me. I wept while I sang, and thus all the leaders wept with me. The inquisitive look in my priestess' eyes turned threatening. She scolded me more harshly than she had ever before: "Stop that!"

My heart's effusion, however, proved the more powerful impetus and the suzerainty of longing the stronger, because I have learned from my struggle that man's exterior is a shadow, and his interior longing, a longing that stirs only when the spirit world dispatches it as a messenger to notify us of our true nature. Even so, we frequently lose sight of our true nature, because we do not listen carefully to the voice of our longing or sing the hymn of our longing properly. Our longing is precisely our identity, which we have forgotten how to discover and which we cannot find any stratagem to retrieve. Why can't singing be that stratagem? Why shouldn't tunes become our prophecy?

Nevertheless, the prophecy that the spirit world whispered to my heart differed from the one the priestess brandished at me when my song provoked her to fling the gauntlet in my face: "You're making a big mistake!"

5 Evening

THE REALLY BIG MISTAKE I made was to toy with another doll beside my wife. My experience notwithstanding, I did not know that a woman is capable of forgiving her husband the foulest misdeeds and the gravest sins so long as he does not supplant her with a baby doll, since a woman is less threatened by a co-wife than by a doll, which forces her to face the fact that she too is a doll, shaken and exposed to the worst perils. Unfortunately, my yearning for amusement made me forget myself and neglect this secret truth about dolls until later. In the meantime there were some weighty developments. I announced my intentions—in a weakened state, without knowing what I was doing—that the nobles of each clan should play the role of Ragh's descendents, whose duty it is to govern, provided that they eschew worldly vanities, as the law decreed. In my declaration I did not forget to append a proviso cautioning that their appointment was temporary—by the law of entertainment—and highlighting the future role of embryos fidgeting in the wombs. In this way I committed another offense, as I understood only later, for sovereignty is the only treasure that should not be meted out in jest and for entertainment. It is an elusive quality, and anyone with a natural talent for ruling will reject such an arrangement, for even sovereignty conferred in jest becomes a reality, no matter how fraudulent its origin.

In feverish longing I raised my voice and uttered a second proclamation to the effect that the nobles of the other tribes would assume the role of the goddess Yeth's community, whom the law burdens with ownership of material goods. It would be their duty to select a descendant of Ragh to ascend the throne, someone devoid of desires for material possessions. Then longing swept through me as melodies wailed in my heart and I uttered the final words of the proclamation, declaring that the blacksmiths, who had slipped into the oasis one day from the east, would assume the role of Seth's offspring, who excel in metalworking, mixing of alloys, and creating iron and other hard substances. Then a weakness of a type familiar to anyone who has felt the pains of longing overwhelmed me. So I lay down and drew a cover over my head, thinking I had said what I needed to say. I do not know how long I was unconscious, but when I awoke I found my slave Hur standing by my head. He said that two men, who were flinging accusations at each other and calling each other names, were waiting at my door, demanding to see me. I granted them permission to enter and found myself confronted by two fellows veiled with dark leather. Their eyes, which looked stern and stubborn, showed lingering anger. The men were similar enough to have been twins, except that they were of different heights. The taller one spoke. He said he had entrusted his friend with some gold dust on the understanding that it would be handed back once he returned from his voyage to the forest lands, but that the cunning strategist had betrayed him by molding the powder into a vile ingot, which he had created and refused to surrender. He asked me to settle their dispute with justice rather than let it be settled by the sword.

He fell silent, and I looked at his shorter companion, whom I asked bluntly, "Do you deny this?"

He shook his head "no."

"Do you admit that the gold belongs to your companion?" I asked him.

He answered without any hesitation, "Certainly!"

"So why have you denied him what is rightfully his?"

"I don't deny that the gold dust is rightfully his. I deny his right to what he refers to as a 'vile ingot.'"

"What do you mean?"

"I mean I don't deny that I owe him a handful of gold dust, but that doesn't mean I owe him an ingot to which I entrusted my spirit as my hands created it."

"If you don't want to give him back the ingot you love, why don't you return some gold dust?"

"Master, I've asked him to allow me more time to acquire some gold dust, but he wants to claim the ingot instead of the gold dust."

"Did you ask his permission before you smelted his gold dust into your ingot?"

"How could I ask his permission, master, when he had traveled far away?"

"Did he not tell you when to expect him back?"

"Absolutely not!"

"But what gave you the right to violate a trust bestowed upon you?"

"Master, when I looked at the gold dust, I saw it was beautiful. When I gazed into my heart, I realized I was in love."

"I really don't understand."

So the lover narrated the story of his infatuation as he gazed off into space: "I responded to an inner call, after I acquainted myself with the look of the gold dust, for I found its gleam seductive. Then I poured the powder into the furnace one night when an unfamiliar fever tormented me. I didn't discover I

had created an antidote for this fever until I shaped the powder and turned it into poetry. Yes, indeed, I created poetry
from dirt, master."

"Would you be willing to show me this poetry?"

He began to stare through the doorway leading to the vacant
lands outside. His eyes also looked vacant. No, a frightening
anxiety flared in his eyes along with another inner call? A sign?
Passion? Latent anxiety? I do not know, but when he finally
overcame his hesitation and decided to withdraw the treasure
from his garment his hand trembled. He extracted a leather con-
tainer from the sleeve of his gown. He clung tightly to this with
both hands for some time, before relenting and presenting it to
me. I accepted the object and withdrew from the wrapper what
his irate comrade had referred to as the "vile ingot." It was a
physical creation of a unique, lustrous appearance: strange, rich,
with an inner beauty and glory. The metal did not reveal its
beauty or glory; these spoke through its solid form the way priests
speak through a curtain. They were diffused throughout the
metal's being, where they created an existence the body denied
them. Through secrecy, concealment, and absence, beauty and
glory revealed themselves completely, becoming existent, alive,
and eternal. Was this a metal idol or a sacred shrine? Was this
masterpiece a metal rod or the body of a goddess?

Impressed, I asked the love-struck man, "Is this a devotional
object?"

His eyes looked off into the distance once more. When I
repeated my question, he replied murkily, "The ingot is me,
master."

"What?"

"Before me, master, rests my heart."

I resumed my contemplation of his creation. As I turned it over
in my hands, I discovered that it was almost painfully smooth.

Soon a whispered temptation stirred in my own breast, a temptation awakened by the spirit world, which permeated the golden
masterpiece. I felt I had seen it before, even though I was certain
this was the first time the object had fallen into my hands. Where?
When? I tried to squeeze certainty from my memory as I once had
when the unknown cast me on the heights above Targa, leaving
me to experience forgetfulness. This time, however, the prophecy
was blocked, notwithstanding the delight I felt in losing myself in
the beauty that flowed through the lustrous body—like the spirit
flowing through a person's body—and in the pleasure I experienced in pursuing its glory, which hid to reveal itself the better and
concealed itself to grow stronger. What spirit lay concealed within this metal? What god was camouflaged by this glorious body?

I kept turning the shrine over in my hands. Finally I said,
"You have the right to refuse to surrender the ingot, and your
companion has the right to receive the gold dust he entrusted
to you."

"I begged him, master, to give me a little time."

I turned to ask his comrade, "Will you give him a little
more time?"

He replied without any hesitation, "Absolutely not!"

I gazed at the love-struck man and said regretfully, "There's
no way around it. You'll have to give him the devotional object
in exchange for his gold dust."

"Absolutely not!"

I looked sadly at him and asked, "Do you know that a person
who trifles with a trust faces the same penalty as one who
defaults on a loan?"

"I know!"

"Do you know the penalty for defaulting on a loan under to
the law of the oasis?"

"I know!"

"Would you rather deliver yourself to him as his slave than deliver the metal ingot?"

"This body's not merely a metal ingot, master."

"I won't deny its perfection, but what you term a body is an ingot in the eyes of the law."

"I told you, master, that body is me."

"What good will retaining possession of your handiwork do you if the law punishes you by making you a slave?"

"I will pledge him my body, pursuant to the verdict, but it's inconceivable that he should take the pledge I've concealed within the body that lies before me, master."

I reflected a little before asking him, "Will you tell me the divine object's secret, if I pardon you?"

The lover merely gazed off into the distance without replying.

I returned the devotional object to him and sentenced him to be his companion's slave for several years. They departed, hurling insults at one another and calling each other names, as my slave Hur later told me. I tried to forget these two wretched adversaries and to drive the whole confused muddle from my mind, but the inspiration of the extraordinary devotional object flowed through my heart the same way the goddess' unknown beauty flowed through that metal rod. I tried to discover its secret. I slept for a long time, roamed in dreams for a long time, and attempted to adjudicate many disputes fairly, but the divine object's secret remained a mysterious talisman that never left my heart. One day I was chatting with my consort, who was seated in the chamber beside me. She was gazing out of the palace window toward the open countryside in a way that I found inspirational, and this awakened in my heart a missing sign. The sensation troubled me, and so I went to the caves of the ancestors with a few vassals. There, in the refuge of the original prophetic wisdom, revelation flowed forth and the prophecy that I had awaited and that had escaped me for such a long time trickled into my heart. In a moment, I discovered that the devotional object the wretch had created was a goddess and, in fact, the priestess herself. Yes, yes, the goddess smelted into the golden rod was none other than my consort in worldly matters, my intimate in our chamber, my sister by blood, and my priestess in the temple. Why had it taken me so long to discern the similarity?

I ordered the vassals to fetch the miserable lover at once. When he appeared, I asked him to show me the divine object again. He wept, alleging that he had lost the treasure, but his comrade, who now owned him, denied this, saying the vile fellow had hidden the goddess in some safe place, for fear greedy people would plot to steal it. The lover, however, attacked the other man, saying he was not satisfied with gaining possession of him through the verdict but intended to seize control of the goddess as well. A quarrel flared up between them, and their anger reached such heights that they flung accusations at one another and called each other names. I was going to order the two men fettered and left out in the sun till they calmed down, but instead, set them free and sent spies after them to keep me posted about what they did and where they went. These spies eventually returned to tell me that the owner was also spying on his slave, in hopes of learning where the devotional object was hidden but that the love-struck man was the more clever of the two, for they had seen him mix suspect herbs into his master's food so the fool would doze off and sleep like a log all night long. Meanwhile the wretch would slip off to the northern, sandy, cliff faces to retrieve his doll, to which he would whisper in a tongue like jinn's gibberish, continuing till dawn. They also informed me they had tried to find the treasure and had dug through the earth there repeatedly without discovering the trophy. I told myself that the lover hid his worshiped object in the endless sands, where he would find it easily the next time, since he held the landmarks in his heart, not in his visual memory, whereas such signs would be invisible to the heart of anyone searching with his eyes. I grasped this secret and then ordered them to pounce on the wretch during his whispered conversations and to bring me the goddess. In a few days they delivered what I wanted. As I contemplated it, I found that its resemblance to the goddess of the temple had increased. I was astonished I had missed this the previous time. I probed it, examined it, and attempted to extract the poetry from its essence. Beauty spoke so clearly in its bearing and glory was so radiantly diffused through its structure that I felt choked and tears flowed from my eyes. The longing I had not experienced in the refrains of the songs touched me. I began to confide in the goddess object daily, because I enjoyed it more than the priestess in whose image it was forged. Was this miracle caused by passion? Does love create what the human will cannot? Does passion devise what the intellect cannot?

I hid the body in a secure place and was therefore incredulous when I discovered the treasure missing a few days later. The adored body disappeared from my safekeeping just as its lover disappeared from the safekeeping of the entire oasis. They searched for him in the caves, on the cliff faces, and in the nearby pasture lands, but the wretch had vanished. I lamented the loss of my adored, golden object for some time until I found consolation with my real-life object of adoration. It never once occurred to me that the loss of the devotional image was a harbinger of ill and a warning that I might lose the original as well. All the same, a series of events began to unfold in my oasis that day. My true love first disappeared from the bedchamber. Originally, her excuse was some feminine complaint. I thought she was expecting a second child, but the signs of pregnancy did not appear.

Instead of witnessing her return to the bedchamber, I was flabbergasted when she moved out of the palace altogether and sought refuge in the temple, spending her nights there. When I asked why, she cited an emptiness of heart, saying that this was a threat from the spirit world and that the only antidote was singing hymns of grief and seeking refuge in the sanctuary. I heard her sing those immortal songs that caused stone to crumble and birds to fall dead to the ground from delight and that had once enchanted the sages, who had summoned her to be the temple's goddess. At first, she withdrew there alone, but later I found that her maids and servants had joined her and had begun spending their nights in the temple. So doubts troubled me. I detected in my slave Hur's eyes a sorrow I ought to have deciphered but did not, because lassitude spawns intellectual apathy and spiritual ruin. Thus I chose to ignore his sorrow, attributing the whole affair to the bizarre phases of this mysterious community known as women. I once went to recite a psalm of longing inside the sanctuary, where she accosted me at the entrance. I gazed into her eyes, but she turned away. The enchanting way she turned to gaze into the distance reminded me of the immortal look flowing through the body of the lost devotional object. She seemed privy to eternity's secret, which lay beyond the horizon. Pain tormented my heart, but I asked her, "Punishment obeys a law, and according to the legal code of the ancients the culprit is entitled to learn the complete charges against him."

Avoiding my gaze, she said, "The culprit was fully informed of the charge a long time ago, but the plaintiff has not been granted the defendant's undivided attention."

"I just don't get it."

At that she turned toward me and then I saw another woman in her eyes. She said defiantly, "The day you set aside for entertainment, didn't compassion's shadow scream, asking you to stop? Didn't the voice of prophecy shout in your ears to warn you that you were making a big mistake, the day you set aside for entertainment?"

I stared at her with genuine astonishment. Stunned, I asked, "Is it reasonable for the earth to quake just because one action figure wants to play with another? Does it make sense for the sky to fall just because one shadow gives offense by wishing to joke around with other shades?"

Pallor spread over her cheeks and the sparkle left her eyes. I thought she was going to faint. With the language of a priestess prophesying, she declared, "You really don't know what you did. You don't know that you mixed the sacred with the defiled. You don't know that you betrayed prophetic counsel and shook the pillars of existence. You. . . ."

She stopped. She sighed, and her sigh sounded like the hissing of a serpent. She tried to finish, but anger choked her. In her eyes I saw an even more hideous gleam. Was it contempt? What was certain, however, was that this look was a message instructing me that I had lost her forever, because a woman can hide everything except her decision to leave a man.

At that time I stood nervously by the temple's entrance. I stood there nervously because I did not understand. I forgot my intention to pray. The longing in my heart to encounter the spirit world faded. I stood where I was, dumbstruck, because I found myself an accused man on whom a death sentence has been pronounced, even though he does not know the nature of his offense. I perceived, intuitively, that something had happened. The conspiracy hatched in the spirit world had begun to mature. I remembered the lost goddess then. I considered it an ill omen and felt hurt. I did not know that this was only the opening volley in the bloodshed that would follow after the "big mistake" but before the breach.

The nobles of the tribes had grown accustomed to gathering in my assembly to represent the divine trinity Ragh, Yeth, and Seth, according to the dictates of the prophetic teachings, recorded on leather sheets that the sages had left me. They launched their first raid against the neighboring tribes on a troubling pretext. The public reason was self-defense against the greed of envious persons, whereas the private subtext was a desire to seize herds of animals and to extend their area of influence. The cavalry, composed of partisans of the goddess Yeth, were the most ardent and the most vociferous advocates of war. I heard their nobles stress in the assembly a heretical idea, the gist of which was that the noblest form of defense is a pre-emptive strike and that a weapon that remains in a person's hand will end up in his throat, unless used against an enemy. With this vicious doctrine they were secretly alluding to the deadly metal blades with which blacksmiths, partisans of Seth, were flooding the markets of the oasis. Among the citizens, they circulated rumors that advocated the necessity of using weapons, if only as a training exercise, since in their opinion, iron formed into weapons is not really a weapon, until used as one. I noticed during the nobles' debate, which preceded the agreement to wade into the first clash, that those from the tribes of Seth were covertly supporting the position of the cavalry of Yeth, by an occasional wink and by repeating prophetic dicta that laud aggression and say that life is merely a voyage of struggle, during which you are inevitably conquered by other people, unless you conquer them first. I heard them allege repeatedly that these dicta were copied from the laws of the ancients. The tribal lords, who had assumed the role of the partisans of Ragh back on the day set aside for entertainment, opposed them and advocated a wait-and-see approach, pleading for the rule of wisdom. They said that wisdom is iron's ancient enemy, that these two have never united under a single roof, and that tribes have noticed, since the beginning of time, that the appearance of one entails the disappearance of the other, because wisdom flows from the spring of peace-making, whereas iron flows exclusively from the spring of blood. I remember that back then the tribe of Seth adopted the position of the tribe of Yeth when the moment came to vote for the first attack. Then their alliance was disclosed and intellect lost the first battle.

My assembly still met whenever necessary. My consort would sit beside me without volunteering any opinion. She seemed bored by all the assembly's wrangling, which often deteriorated into name-calling, and began to absent herself. When I once asked why, she replied, "I didn't know that men's meetings, when drawn out, become even more mean-spirited than women's." When I disputed this, she observed that a man's initial comments deserve to be heard but become pointless chatter if prolonged while his heart becomes a shell. In her head, a woman always conceals in her quiver a valuable thought she does not reveal. Indeed, a woman never states what she would like to say. She never says what she ought to say, because she knows that the thought we treasure is always inestimably more precious than the statement we utter. For this reason, we never grow tired of listening to a woman. For this reason, we are attracted to a woman, since we anticipate that she will eventually tell us the thought she is hiding. Woman, however, is too intelligent to condescend to speak her secret, unlike man. She concluded her exposition by stating, "How despicable is a man who has not been granted wisdom by the spirit world." I realized that she had pronounced a final verdict on my assembly. I also understood that her final phrase, with which she terminated her bizarre exposition, was directed at me, not the nobles of my assembly. Her phrasing

would not have aroused my suspicions had I not detected contempt in it. I must confess that this was what most upset me,
because I knew that when a woman feels contempt for a man,
not even the spirit world can deflect her evil. These intima-
tions shook my heart's optimism; so I learned to be suspicious
and began to read hidden meanings into every phrase. Next
she began to siphon off the leading figures of the assembly,
one by one, until I discovered that they had deserted me to
unite in her assembly in the temple. I was astonished at the
ability of people to change over night and to turn their backs
on me, after I had placed my confidence in them, and to shun
me so unequivocally that they saw nothing wrong in scowling
at me today after kissing the ground beneath my feet yesterday. I confronted a noble from Ragh's clan, a man I had previously installed as the head of his people and a pillar of the
assembly. I decided I would try to reason with him, even
though I had no hope of success. He was a mature man of
great dignity, inclined toward silence. He wore a veil of blue
linen. In fact it was reported in the oasis that he was the first
to substitute for leather veils these linen ones that caravans
procured for him from nations to the north. That was not all,
for he had dyed the linen blue the day after I installed him on
the Trinitarian throne as a representative of the putative offspring of Ragh. When asked his reasons, he had said that
since blue is the color of the sky, it would have been inappropriate for descendents of the divine lords to wend their way
through the throngs without a sign to notify strangers of their
true status as persons tracing their lineage back to the lord of
the sky. Then he pushed his game one step further by decid-
ing to change his name as well, substituting for his former
name, Imsikni, a new one, Amnay. At the time, I did not lend
any significance to these initiatives. All I did was joke about

them in the assembly, just as strangers had previously joked about them. I did not understand then that joking about people is not merely a mistake but also dangerous, for a joke conceals a display of contempt that will provoke the people subjected to it. Then they do not merely harbor hatred for us, but the show of contempt for their position increases their determination to carry out their heretical innovation, even if it verges on the impractical or the insane. Here was Amnay strutting before me as haughtily as a lord, veiled by a blue cloth that idiots assumed was a guarantee of affiliation with descendents of the sky, hiding behind a lofty sobriquet accepted by strangers as having been bestowed on him one night in a heavenly revelation, and leaning on a staff that, in his grasp, became a mace and symbol of sovereignty. Here he was, pretending not to see me, in fact avoiding me, as he had done repeatedly. I blocked his way, not to remind him who he really was, not to avenge myself for his skullduggery, but to heal my rancor and to cheer my heart, as I had attempted to do the day I set aside for amusement, when I had laid the cornerstone for my own downfall, as my former consort was pleased to remind me. I blocked the way of this gent, who was bristling with fine clothing, and asked, without muting the disdain in my tone, "The master of nobility shows himself to people by bristling with wisdom, whereas the master of vacuity reveals himself to people by bristling with lies."

He studied me, while brandishing his mace in the air to mask his discomfort, but never once looked me in the eye. I told myself the man's soul surely retained some remnant of shame. Nonetheless, he said, with the glibness of a man proficient in double-talk, "Do we know, master, anything about the stronghold of reality? Do we know, master, anything about the stronghold of falsehood? What can show us, master, that the stronghold of reality is in the homeland of falsehood? What can show us, master, that the stronghold of falsehood is in the homeland of reality?"

"Should I be surprised to hear an exposition like this from a man who claims to be a prophet?"

"On the contrary, master! My master will never hear an exposition of this from anyone except a prophet."

"Is that so?"

The cunning strategist, however, waved his stick in the air and continued to recite his prophecy without looking me in the eye: "Absolutely! I'm not cognizant of the reality of reality nor of the reality of falsehood, because this type of knowledge is found only in the spirit world, but I do know that reality cannot be established without falsehood and that falsehood cannot be established without reality. Had this not been the case, our master would never have needed to jest one day."

"Bravo! Bravo! Here you are talking about the jest that made you a ruler. Then you disavow this regime and its ruler."

"I meant to say that the fraud we term 'jest' is the same fraud that creates reality."

"Do you label your situation at present 'reality'?"

"Isn't our present situation the actual one that we can see and touch?"

"Do you take everything seen to be real?"

"What does my master consider everything seen?"

"I would have thought the reverse. I would have thought that the fraudulent is what is seen and the reality what's not seen."

"If my master is right, what meaning is there to all this? What meaning is there to debating? What meaning is there to loving? What meaning is there to living?"

"Yes, indeed; there is no meaning to living. The meaning is, rather, in learning to live."

"This is the language of the law!"

"I would have thought that the master of prophetic visions would be, of all the people, the worthiest person with whom to discuss a clear exposition of the law."

"Not so fast! Not so fast, master."

I did not cut him any slack. I did not go slow with him, for I decided to render a verdict: "I fraudulently installed you as my replacements. Then you betrayed me to install yourselves for real. Is this legal according to your law, which celebrates what is visible?"

He replied icily, "Certainly, master. This is a legal system for what is visible. We, master, are the children of what is visible."

"I thought I heard you discuss your affiliation with offspring of the spirit world."

"Certainly; I am a scion of the spirit world, and it is, my master, the spirit world that has decreed that I should live according to the law of what's visible, for there is a wisdom I do not understand in the fact that it plucked me from the hidden recesses of the spirit world to place me in the homelands of light."

"Amazing!"

"What's amazing, master, is that we live in the physical world according to the spirit's laws of the private and live in spirit world according to the laws for public life."

"From now on, I won't be surprised if you all rule in favor of aggression and seek to enslave the members of pacific tribes. I've even begun to wonder if you're the mastermind behind the schemes of aggression."

"Yes, certainly, master; the mind plotting what you term aggression is mine and the law of visible reality is what has inspired me to spread the influence of the oasis beyond its boundaries, because the spirit world does not grant a community wealth, sovereignty, or wisdom to fool around with, the way numbskulls do, but to use in visible ways. If we don't master the tribes of the world with our power today, they'll enslave us tomorrow, when our powers have waned, for the spirit world's law has hidden its secret in an endlessly revolving wheel. This is an inexorable wheel that reclaims today what it created yesterday and resurrects tomorrow what it assassinates today."

I listened to him dumbfounded, because from this terrifying jinni's discourse I learned that this was not just a plot against me but a conspiracy against the entire desert and that my wife was not the mastermind plotting this insurrection but merely a piece of the snare the cunning strategist had disclosed to me in his fatal exposition.

After this, nothing surprised me. I was not surprised when the nobles deserted me, one at a time. I was not surprised when they clustered around my former consort in the temple's heart to finish weaving the strands of this conspiracy. I was not surprised when they kept me from seeing my son, preventing me from sharing stages of his development as he grew, matured, and explored the desert, where he learned to hunt, grew tough, and discovered how to be a man. I found myself alone, isolated, and abandoned, just as I had always been. I grew ever more certain that the fate of men in this desert is always Anubi's. I was born in the desert like Anubi, live in the desert like Anubi, and will leave the desert one day the way Anubi did, for anyone whose father has ever left him will have Anubi's destiny as his eternal fate. My slave Hur attempted to lighten my burden. "What's all this, my master, but a trial from which we can learn?" he asked me one day.

"Learn what, Hur?"

"Learn the reality of truth and falsehood."

"Don't talk to me about the reality discussed by the prophet of lying."

"The prophet of lying?"

"Is the leader of the people of Ragh anything other than the lie's prophet?"

"Master, we'll never recognize truthful prophets, if we aren't plagued by the lying ones."

"But I lost reality the day I decided to play. I have come to believe that the lady of the temple was right to scold and menace me with the punishment appropriate to this offense."

"We can't learn, master, unless we suffer."

"I lost reality, thanks to my taste for amusement; so forgive me."

"Despair master, is also therapeutic."

"I have lost my offspring, my nation, and my reality and have brought you all down with me. Worse than all this is the fact that I've lost my son. By losing the prophetic counsel of the law, I lost my son."

"We don't find ourselves, if we don't lose ourselves, master."

"The one thing I ask from you is to refrain from changing my offspring's name. Inform the people that as of today my name is no longer Ara. From today forward it will be Amahagh; so don't forget."

"We are all Imuhagh, master. We are all children of a desert labyrinth. None of us, master, knows what to do with himself. It is this ignorance that motivates us to commit offenses like playing, because we must inevitably ask ourselves one day: 'What will we do with ourselves, if we don't play?' Thus entertainment slays us, just as others are slain by longing. One group dies from the offense of playing, master, and another group dies from the disease of longing."

"I entrust my offspring Imuhagh to your care and count on you to divulge to all the people the true nature of this name."

"Master, I pledge my life to be true to this trust."

A few days later I was informed of the community's verdict, which sentenced me to exile, once more.

6   The Slip

I FOUND MYSELF in my desert, cleansing myself with the last drops of my mirage and roaming through the endless expanse of my open countryside. I returned to my solitude and believed in my solitude, since only solitude is real. The evidence for this claim is that within its confines I had no need for entertainment in order to live. I discovered life-threatening entertainment to be an innovation created by the lassitude of oases. The antidote to this malady is closer to us than the jugular vein, since it rushes to greet us as soon as we venture into the desert, embracing us to provide a replacement for whatever we have left behind. I roamed and began, in the labyrinth, to purify myself. I contemplated what appeared and what was concealed, what was manifest and what latent, what was visible and what invisible, and cleansed myself from all the rot of lethargy. I stood a foot or less from a sanctuary to the spirit world, feeling certain that if I called out, I would receive a response and that if I pressed my intrusion an inch farther it would appear before me. Yet, fearful, I suppressed my cry each time, so that I would not receive an answer, and confined my intrusive behavior to my head, so it would not show. I quit my confrontations with the covert and diverted myself by reading the talismans of the ancients on the rock statues or on the walls of the caves or by re-enacting my first gallop behind the herds of gazelles or pursuit of the heads of

Barbary sheep, when the fates cast me at the outskirts of the oasis. Then I had eaten my relatives' flesh grilled by a heavenly lightening bolt, and my body has been aflame with greed ever since. I roamed through the companionable countryside. I rambled around to enjoy my isolation, reveling in the time I had alone with my beloved, whom I realized I had betrayed when I substituted for her another creature, who soon betrayed me. I courted my former true love with the most heart-rending poetry. I sang her plaintive ballads she had never heard before, not even from the jinn's female vocalists, whom I had seen in the caves and encountered while they roamed the great outdoors by the full moon. I forgot my curse. I forgot my destiny. I forgot Anubi's fate, which had always encumbered me. I forgot my lost father. I forgot the lost law. I forgot my lost spouse. I forgot my lost oasis. I forgot my lost reality, for the desert became father, law, spouse, homeland, and reality for me. I threw myself into its embrace. Then it eased my mind, dandled me, calmed me, and made me forget my exhaustion. I wandered through its vast expanses. I scaled peaks to discover springs that my desert had never shown any creature before. I descended ravines and valleys to find, in their lowest reaches, wells that my consort had hidden from strangers' eyes for ages. When I wandered across the plains, she fed me secret fruit more delicious than any I had ever tasted. My desert showed me her affection like a tender mother with an errant child, a son who returns after a misguided voyage. So how could I help but recite poems about her beauty or sing ballads glorifying her?

My former true love was not content to celebrate my return with all this munificence; she sent my way some jinn disguised as people to console me and to dispel from my heart the isolation that mankind terms loneliness. Then she sent my way people masquerading as jinn to show me how remorseless people are. The most precious treat she granted me was the hint of purity that drew me close to my secret reality, however, for it was this exalted purity that brought me to a stop only a fraction of an inch from the sanctuary where I felt that, were I to call, I would be granted a response invisible to human eyes, inaudible to human ears, and unimaginable by the human mind. The past's pains, with which the desert had once weighed me down to test me and to make a man of me, became the memory of a comforting grace. The delights of lethargy, which the oasis had generously showered upon me, became the memory of a hideous inferno. I saw how hell frequently is transformed into a blessing when it becomes a memory, and a blessing frequently evolves into an inferno in memory; the talisman, apparently, is a pawn to the riddle named time, which deliberately puts us off, delays us, and fails to inform us of the true nature of what transpires on a certain day until it is too late.

I was entranced by this healing and felt myself light as a straw, as pure as a tear; like a person recovering from a lengthy, near fatal illness. I smiled, because I understood that the group of conspirators, who had thought they were harming me, had actually done me a favor. Nonetheless, the nightmare of the oasis soon swept over my solitude to disrupt my blessing and to ruin my situation. Are the wise men of the tribes correct when they say that the spirit world's envy does not allow anyone's happiness to last long?

I did not hear the news that troubled me from an emissary or a messenger but from a wayfarer, who casually mentioned it during a night he spent with me before heading north the next day. I met up with him near the edge of the extensive Tinghart desert on the threshold of a terrifying tomb of the type that the ancients customarily built for their chiefs, leaders, dignitaries, and priests. I buried under the ashes of the fire some gray-colored truffles I had gathered during my wanderings in a valley that had received autumn rain from a fickle cloud. As soon as the wayfarer sniffed the fragrance of the truffles, he went into an ecstatic trance and began to moan like a suffering patient. When I pulled out this treasure and set it before him, he gazed at the legendary comestible for a long time. Then, without ever ceasing his mysterious moaning, he started to examine each section with as much curiosity as a diviner hunting for a portent. He did not reveal his secret to me until after midnight. At first he sang about an oasis named Targa. I did not know whether he was singing about my lost oasis or about the Targa that generations have celebrated in the epic songs of the ancestors and that the tribes, so long ago that no one remembers, had lost, so that its name was given by sages to any country that one cannot hope to visit and live to return from. Finally he concluded his song by saying that any legend we believe will become a reality, even if originally it was a fiction, and that whatever a creature covets in the unseen world will be presented to him by the spirit world in the visible world, and that the proof for this is the oasis of Targa, for the desert nations have never seen anything comparable to it. Then, out of the blue, he asked, "Have you heard about the magician who created an image of the lady of the temple from gold and thus mastered her spirit?"

"They say he created the image out of love for beauty," I answered. "But he fled from the oasis for fear something would happen to a creation to which he had entrusted his spirit."

"Yes, in the solid metal two spirits met: the lady's spirit and the spirit of the creator of the lady."

"I like that!"

"Because the law of the gods, according to the lore of these magicians, is creation of a creature, and the law of the creature is the creation of the gods, and the creator's creation is artistic creation. This harbors the secret. Here is hidden the insane passion."

"How creative this is! Are you a poet?"

He did not answer my question. Sprawled out beside me in the open air, he spoke as if confiding to the stars or addressing himself: "The lord of the oasis thought the lady's lover had fled from the oasis, but would a lover ever flee from his true love? Does the creature flee from his creator? Or the creator from his creation? Far from it!"

"The wretch didn't flee from the oasis?"

"The lover does not flee from the beloved he has created in his spirit even before his hands shape it. The lover does not flee from his beloved, because the lover is the beloved's destiny, just as the creator is his creation's destiny. The lady pulled the rug out from under the feet of the lord of the oasis, because he had given her power but had been stingy with creativity. She threw herself into the embrace of the lover who created her, because he had invented her."

"What do you mean by saying that the lord of the oasis gave his wife power but stinted on creativity?"

"I meant to say that the ruler gave his wife an oasis but did not give her a heart, whereas the homeland for a woman is a heart, not a land. The fault of the ruler lay in forgetting that woman flees from a wealthy man who gives her a kingdom if he veils his heart from her; and she surrenders herself to a shepherd who offers her a residence outdoors but awards her his heart."

"Woe is the man who feels secure with a woman!"

"It's said that after she expelled her husband from the precincts of the country the lady of the oasis abdicated the throne to her lover."

"Not so fast! Tell me first of all the truth about the lover's disappearance from the oasis."

"The lover didn't disappear from the oasis. The woman hid her beloved in her chamber."

"In her chamber?"

The way I shouted this almost revealed my identity. The fact was that the news rattled me, because like any man who has been betrayed I was so confident of myself I could not believe this. The poet, however, was anything but merciful in his narration: "It's said in the oasis that the priestess seized power after her consort, the ruler, denied her the throne, not because she wanted political power but to guarantee the right of the offspring of the mother to inherit the world and likewise to take vengeance on her cast-off husband."

"Vengeance on her cast-off husband?"

"She wanted revenge on her husband because he, according to accounts, had once upon a time slain her father."

He fell silent, and then I heard in the night's silence the muddled hubbub of roaring jinn. I realized that a creature whom the spirit world abandons will never escape the sword's thrust, not in the farthest reaches of the desert. I tried to eavesdrop on the hubbub in my heart. Then I heard the sojourner prophet continue with his recital: "The creature who fled from the oasis was not the lover but the son."

"The son?"

"The child of the original leader!"

I could hear my own pulse throbbing but asked, "Where did the son flee?"

"To parts unknown, looking for his father."

"Did you say he was looking for his father?"

"Yes, indeed; each of us searches for his father. A son who does not search for his father is not worth much. A son who does not search for his father will never be successful. It's said in the oasis that the boy's father would never have discovered the treasure that is the oasis named Targa, if he had not been searching for his own father."

He fell silent. I soon heard his breathing grow steady and knew he had fallen asleep. Yet, I found no sign of him in the morning. So, even today, I do not know whether my guest that night was the wandering offspring of wayfarers or a spectral messenger of the jinn.

7   False Dawn

THE WANDERER'S PROPHECY about a son who set off in search of his father awakened in my chest a forgotten longing for my child. So I began to hunt for news of his fate, but the vast desert had swallowed him. Wanderers, herdsmen, and leaders of caravans brought me no news of him. Instead, they provided me with information about plots being hatched between key figures in the assembly on the one hand and elite figures in the palace on the other. It was reported that the "Master of the Troop," as he was known by inhabitants of the oasis had chopped off the head of the leader of the sons of Seth, whose intentions he suspected, and that he had chosen a puppet from that tribe to replace him. Then he dismissed the leader of the sons of Yeth from the assembly, as well, for saying too openly that raiding desert tribes was a dangerous adventure that would result in an unnecessary amount of bloodshed. He also replaced him with a puppet from the tribe. He was not content with that but conspired against the lady of the oasis. He abducted her beloved poet, who disappeared without a trace. It was reported that he had killed and then buried him in a rugged area of the southern oasis. Others said he did not bury him but handed him over to the ironworkers to cremate in the smelting furnaces, in order to obliterate all traces. People expected the wily strategist to seize the throne next, but this spurious leader was more cunning than the dolts suspected. He headed for the bedchamber rather than the throne and ruled the oasis from there. He took the priestess for his consort but left her on the throne as a scarecrow, an empty shell, to cast dust in people's eyes. Meanwhile he hid himself behind the scarecrow's body, thus gaining power surreptitiously. The spirit world, however, was eventually victorious, once it took charge of the matter.

Time gushed forth and the oasis' army conquered the desert, but this suzerainty did not last long. As continued raids multiplied the tax burdens of the inhabitants of the oasis, people were ruined, the condition of the oasis was undermined, and the spell rebounded on the sorcerer. The oasis received painful blows, and its influence over the desert diminished gradually. Times looked bleak, and the oasis retreated to a defensive position. Next it lost its ability to defend itself and consented to pay tribute, so the victors' swords would allow people to brood about their rout inside the confines of their shell. I was upset by the fate of my oasis, which had once been known throughout the entire desert for its prosperity and happiness. Tranquil, it had been sheltered from the ravages of time throughout the history of all its generations. Soon after I wondered with a wounded man's passion about the true nature of epochs and about the caprices of time, I received an answer from the desert's shejinni, who visited me in my hermitage one day. Disguised in the ragged clothing of an aged priestess of the southern deserts, she was accompanied by two maids, one of whom clung to her right hand, while the other was hanging onto her left one. Her procession was preceded by coveys of demon spirits masquerading as slaves and by an entourage of servants and vassals. The shejinni took me by the hand and led me away from the others. She told me that just as water evaporates, sand scatters, and stone crumbles, the world has three time periods. Yesterday's time is fraudulent, because no amount of wisdom will suffice to reclaim it. Tomorrow's time is a figment of the imagination, because it has not arrived and perhaps never will, no matter how certain we feel. Today's time is a dream, for we possess no argument that it exists, since its ignobility makes it a bridge, the head of which disappears into what is to happen, whereas its rear end is immersed in what is over and done with. Then she spoke about the nature of the days, saying that each period of time is divisible into units, the heart of which lies in an hour. The hour's heart is in the day. The day's is in what people refer as an age, because this miracle is divisible into twenty-four periods, each of which conceals a life. On concluding with the names of these divisions, she questioned my resolve: "What more than this do you want, man? What do you desire from your world, wretch? Is being born and not being born equivalent for you, scion of futility?" A look of futility was traced on my forehead, glittered in my eye, and encircled my body. Since my destiny seemed to cause her pain, she decided to favor me with a final prophecy: "Those who have lived are not on a par with those who have not, for he who has lived, has lived, even if he has now perished. Someone who was never born, however, leaves behind no memories, trace, or existence. Believe me: the spirit world has been especially compassionate to you. It has favored you, inspired you, entrusted you with its *sententiae*, and granted you a life that has endured for ages, which greedy folk deem the winking of an eye. You have received twenty-three of your life's periods. Once you emerge from the false dawn stage, you'll lack only your morning. If you've learned to live, then you'll have succeeded. If you've failed to learn, you've lost. Know, finally, that loss does not consist in vanishing and passing out of existence but in not knowing how to begin life afresh." Then she turned away, mounted her steed, and rode off.

At that time I had withdrawn into my self. Within my unknown reaches I had dug tunnels, anterooms, and vaults. So I headed for the sanctuary, since I was discovering what I had once discovered on sensing that if I cried out, I would receive a response invisible to the eye, inaudible by the ear, and unimaginable by the human heart. I groped my way from there to guide myself to prophetic aphorisms, wrestle with talismans, and unravel convoluted symbols in order to record in characters the prophetic sayings. I engraved these signs in my heart and bore them for a time deep in my recesses until eventually I found myself inscribing them on solid walls with shards of rock. I toured the caves and explored the caverns so I could confide to solid rock my worries, animating the hard surface with my longing, entrusting to it my truth, and making it a guardian over my life story, which might thus be conveyed to future generations. I also traced what my heart had told me on pieces of leather I branded with fire and hid in many caves. My heart, however, spoke to me of the superiority, trustworthiness, and passion of stone. Therefore I entrusted my heart to stone, which I made the guardian for my passion. I appointed it the trustee for my longing and my revelations, because a whisper informed me that my time was wasting away, that my days were vanishing, and that my morning was nigh.

8   Morning

THE HOSTILE TRIBES tightened their stranglehold over the oasis, and the people suffered cruelly from oppressive taxes. The assembly's specialists in false doctrine learned that there is no turning back for foolhardy persons who have committed evil hastily, for they cannot limit the price of repentance to surrendering and paying tribute to the victor. The price is, rather, unlimited, never-ending submission. This is what happened to the oasis in its risky campaign against neighboring tribes. News reached me of the people's anger and unhappiness with the rule by falsehood's partisans, who treated them to stinging humiliation and doled out bitter hunger to their offspring. Repeated rebellions were brutally suppressed. Nobles of the three tribes assembled, debated, and flung accusations at each other, before they managed to craft a course of action that would protect them, according to their calculations, against the twin evils of being hemmed in by the walls of the oasis and of being attacked by enemies coming from beyond those walls. In keeping with this strategy, they called on each other to advocate a retreat to the surrounding deserts, where they would seek protection from the desert, which has never disappointed anyone who has appealed to it for aid. Thus they would gain a free hand to stave off their enemies and to safeguard the oasis, but from outside. Meanwhile, vassals and agents from the tribes of Seth competed with each other to manage the affairs of the oasis, hiding their actions behind the priestess, that hollow scarecrow.

This game did not, however, alleviate the rancor of the citizens, whose bitter, public demonstrations of anger rocked the oasis, since the tyranny of the spurious doctrine's leader did not end when he moved into the surrounding deserts. In fact, it doubled and reached alarming proportions, thanks to his vassals, disciples, and messengers, not to mention his own secret visits, which he persisted in making, to the palace. He would disguise himself in servants' rags to unite with his doll in the bedchamber and to dictate rules of conduct for the oasis.

With the passing days, however, his vassals, disciples, agents, and even his servants began to grow insolent, for when a game lasts a long time, it ceases to be a game. Weak-spirited people end up mistaking it for reality, and when weak-spirited people mistake a game for reality, it becomes real. So I was surprised one day by the arrival of my former slave Hur, who came as a messenger to me at the head of a troop of mounted men. He told me that the nobles had actually succeeded in protecting the oasis from external attacks but at a cost of battles that had taken many lives. Fending off raids had eaten away at their ranks, destroying many men and leaving only a small corps of survivors. The spurious doctrine's cunning strategist had been slain in his bedchamber at the palace by one of his slaves. When I asked about the fate of the priestess, he bowed his head. A tear slipped from his right eye, before he told me that the mobs had plunged a knife into her throat as well. When I asked about my son, he wept and sighed, before admitting that no trace had been seen of him, ever since the lie's leader had taken control of the palace. He could promise me nothing, although he had not stopped searching. I asked him to say more, but he made it clear he knew only that the boy was determined to reach his father. Then I remembered my destiny and understood that I had passed on to my offspring this unquenchable thirst. Children who do not search for their true nature by tracing their paternal ancestry have little to recommend them. There is no point to a creature that does not seek out its efficient cause. Searching for a father, however, is dangerous. If my son had set out on this path, alas for him, considering all the terrors of the road. He would never be attracted to a sedentary or comfortable life, because his genetic predisposition would be to search, and his daily bread would be a morsel kneaded with suffering. I was consoled to know he truly was my son in whom was borne out the prophecy of the ancient sages, who had one day foretold his destiny to be a seeker who bore in his heart a secret for future generations and a talisman for nations.

A silent despondency gripped the emissaries in deference to my sorrow, and Hur did not dare broach the main topic until after midnight. Then he said that they had come as messengers from the citizens of Targa, who invited me to return as their savior, for they would never accept anyone else as their ruler. He also said that the messengers had been asked to inform me that the oasis, which I had one day accepted as a gift from the spirit world, had, in the course of time, become a bequest for which I was the trustee. To allow it to become a prize snatched at by the hands of dilettantes, swindlers, and adventurers was an offense that could no longer be tolerated. The sages of the oasis when imploring my presence did not wish to weigh me down with the cares of the world but hoped I would agree to lend my authority to their efforts by sitting beside them, since the presence of those who have suffered much, in the opinion of the law, constitutes—in and of itself—wisdom, a protective charm, and a prophetic maxim. They left me no choice but to yield, and I did. I went to the oasis but did not stay in its settlements for long,

because I was overcome by anxiety. Staying in one place suffo-
cated me and left me prey to a lethal depression, from which I
was unable to extricate myself save by resumption of my wandering, nomadic life. I entrusted the oasis to my servant Hur—
advising him to continue the search for my lost child—on condition that he never allow the people to make him their
supreme leader, since anyone who assumes supreme authority
over a people becomes their slave. Only a creature who has
renounced public office can claim control over his self and
befriend the spirit world. A person who has been entrusted with
prophetic counsel will fail unless he breaks away and retreats
from the world. If in time he should find my son, he should
encourage him to travel, because wandering is the fate of anyone destined to search for his father. "Amahagh" was the name
he would bear as a talisman in the world and "Targa" would be
the epithet by which his descendants would be known, for a
prophecy of ancient times revealed that generations of foreign-
ers would use the adjective "Targi" to refer to the nation, thinking this auspicious. Some peoples pronounce this "Tarqi" and
others "Ṭarqi," without knowing that it is Anubi's curse to live
among mankind as a stranger.

I returned to my solitude where its passages received me and
brought home to me the true nature of my situation. I plunged
far down tunnels, extracting from the depths spiritual treasures
I carved on the bodies of the rocks. I did not cease searching
until at last a shadowy apparition obscured by the darkness of
night stood over my head, after arriving on foot. He was of slender build and gloomy coloring, tall, veiled by a well-worn scarf,
covered with dust, and wrapped in a faded garment, which was
also well worn. In his eyes, too, I detected a gloomy expression.
No, no, that was not it. It was not gloom I detected in his eyes
but the determined look of perpetual wanderers. No, that was

not it. It was not the determination of perpetual wanderers but the suffering of exiles. Yes, that was right. It was the misery of those condemned to unending exile, the misery of searchers who have gone astray, the misery of those touched by longing, the misery of those confused by dreams, visions, and poetry, the misery of troubled people who have come to the desert, where they live as strangers, who find nothing better to do with themselves in this world than to flee and to keep moving. It was the misery of that mysterious community in whose veins flows Anubi's blood. Yes, that was it. This wretch standing before me, as perplexed, apprehensive, and hesitant as if he were waiting for an opportunity to flee from my presence toward eternity, was none other than Anubi's child.

He began to tremble as he begged, "A sip of water! Can you spare me a sip of water?"

I hurried to the nearby boulder and fetched a water-skin, which was half full. He grabbed it from me roughly but did not put the mouth of the water-skin to his mouth. Instead, he clung to it with both hands and began to scrutinize me with a vacant but determined look. I realized that he was battling his thirst. He was struggling, with a heroism seen in the desert only among perpetual voyagers who have long familiarity with thirst. Only a person who has had firsthand experience of thirst knows that for a thirsty person to resist his desire for water is more heroic than for a cavalryman to charge toward death's portal, because only those with firsthand experience of thirst understand that thirst is death. Indeed, it is a fate worse than death.

He took his time. He grinned. In his eye gleamed a smile that had forced itself upon him and seemed improvised, as if he were apologizing to me. He seemed to be asking my forgiveness for bursting into my life and spoiling my solitude. Then, however, he looked gloomy again and the glint of eternal suffering flashed in his eyes. Then I saw him bring the water-skin to his mouth. His faded garment slipped down his lean forearms, which resembled sticks of firewood. My heart overflowed with compassion, not just for him but for me as well, and not only for me but for all the creatures of the desert. It was compassion for man, who came to earth to strive, leaving his heart behind him in some homeland, only to find himself suspended, gazing at the horizon that offers glad tidings of a homeland. It is, however, a horizon that does not fulfill its promise, for every horizon opens onto another. Man, therefore, searches for a reality beyond space in order to extinguish his empty belly's insatiable appetite, or thirst, for his lost treasure. Who are you, man? Where are you heading, man?

He swallowed the water slowly, haughtily, and patiently, even though he craved water intensely. Then he suddenly stopped drinking. He stopped before he had drunk his fill, seized the mouth of the water-skin, and cast me a look requesting a tie. I handed him a strip of leather, and he tied it round the mouth of the water-skin, which he retained. I had him sit down by my kit and brought out some dates. He stared at the plate but did not take a single one. In a murky voice he said, "I've got to go."

Without meaning to, I voiced a question that was racing through my heart, tormenting me: "Where to?"

"Hope lies in keeping moving."

I felt certain that Anubi's destiny reverberated in this wanderer's heart. So I mused: "That's the voice of longing. I bet I hear the voice of longing."

"We are all victims of longing."

"What's the use of moving about, since the desert is hospitable to hungry people but crowds out people hungry with longings?"

"Even so, we crave no other fate for ourselves than longing."

"You're right. If granted the choice, we would certainly choose longing."

"I have to leave."

I felt fond of him and feared his leaving. My affection was stronger than that of one descendant of Anubi for another. It was stronger than the affection of an exile for his fellow exile, because the affection aroused by longing, it would seem, is the affection of a unique breed. A person governed by an unfulfilled longing finds refreshment only with a fellow sufferer.

I tried to slow his departure, but he expressed his determination: "I have a long trip ahead of me."

"You must understand that no matter how far you journey, you will never satisfy your longing."

"The longing we satisfy is not really longing. Hope, master, lies in the road, not in the destination."

His language awakened my admiration, and my heart became ever more attached to him. I resolved to search for some other excuse to detain him, if only for a night. I did not realize, until then, that a hankering for anything other than unfulfilled longing is an offense against longing and against ourselves. Clear vision, however, is never possible until it is too late. I committed a fatal error by dispensing with the language of gesture and insinuation. I resorted to the clear expression typical of the masses when I revealed the treasure that I ought to have concealed in my heart: "Don't parents have a right to enjoy the company of their descendants for a night?"

He stared at me with loathing. He seemed not to have understood, for he clung to his silence. I ought to have taken his disapproval as a warning. I should have stopped in my tracks but found myself tripping farther down the road that would lay bare my secret: "Will you spend the night with me if I tell you who I am?"

By the light of the newly full moon I detected in his eyes an even stranger gleam. I saw astonishment, dismay, and pain there. He did not answer my question, and so I moved closer to him: one step, two steps. I leaned over his head and, in the voice one might use on discovering a well or a spring, I yelled: "You're Ara! I'm sure you're Ara!"

In the wink of an eye, everything went topsy-turvy. The slender apparition jumped up from his lair as quick as a demon jinni and trembled in a way I had never seen a creature's body shake before. I could only compare it to the bodies of ecstatic people long tormented by passionate love. I don't know what happened after that for certain. I simply caught sight of the blade of the knife bathed in the light of the newly full moon. Then . . . there was the warmth of the sticky, gooey liquid that was pouring from my neck. I was still on my feet, facing him when I croaked: "But . . . why? Why have you killed me?"

I heard him reply, "Because you'll disclose my secret to people if I don't. Forgive me!"

I pressed my hand to my throat. I felt dizzy, but the blow to my heart was far more severe than that to my body. Defying death, I said: "Don't you know that you've . . . that you've killed your father?"

"Rubbish! Many men have claimed to be my father."

"Prophecy is credible only when we deem it a falsehood. I am your father!"

"Rubbish!"

"Is the son destined to slay his father?"

"Each one of us, master, is created to slay his father. Who among us does not seek his father? Who among us does not wish to slay his father?"

I recognized in his phrase a prophecy that appealed to me. I fought off my vertigo and stuffed a bit of my veil in my wound.

I sat down upon the ground. I decided to utter my prophecy too: "We must slay our father in order to search for our father. We must slay our father in order to find our father."

I heard him repeat my words as if fascinated: "We must slay our father in order to search for him. We must slay our father in order to find him."

"Do you know that one day your father did to his father what you have done to yours today?"

He did not reply. The disk of the full moon began to shimmer and to grow dark in my eye, as I favored the shadowy apparition with my final aphorism. "Here's a bit of advice for you: never raise your hand against a man from whose hand you've taken a sip of water."

He disappeared. I found myself abandoned, left to my stillness as always. My greatest fear was that I would not be able to start a fire to provide enough light so I could complete the final scrap of my life story, which I now understood was not the real truth. My insane desire to transform dream into reality endowed me with sufficient strength to struggle until I was able to light a fire and then trace on a square of leather a final symbol that would provide evidence for future generations of the reality of Anubi, who was neither a shade nor a figment of the imagination but a man, who once crisscrossed the desert.

Part Four
Aphorisms of Anubis

In much wisdom is much grief; and the greater a person's wisdom, the greater his sorrow.

Ecclesiastes 1: 18

WHEN WE SCORN a friend's advice we act according to an enemy's.

Woman resists man's seductions only to submit, whereas man risks his life seducing a woman only to withdraw.

The homeland is a phoenix, for its body is in the sultan's hands, but its spirit lives in the poet's heart.

We surrender ourselves to a minor death, which we call "sleep" and which can renew our life for another day, whereas we reject the major sleep we term "death," even though this might renew our life for eternity.

Stars are pinpricks of conscience in the heart of the sky. Pinpricks of conscience are stars in man's heart.

Frequently what a woman finds attractive in a man also causes their separation.

Ignoble people are born children and die as men. Noble people are born men and die children.

Even hell, once it is only a memory, becomes pleasant.

Some pleasant things, similarly, turn into hellish memories.

Patriots boast of their affiliation with a homeland. The desert dweller boasts of his affiliation with nonexistence.

The desert is a paradise of nonexistence.

For the body, the desert is a place of exile, whereas for the spirit, the desert is a paradise.

Water cleanses the body, but the desert cleanses the soul.

For us to withdraw from the world is heroic. For the world to withdraw from us is disgraceful.

Once desire stirs, the appreciation of beauty ends.

The bodies of mothers become bloated from bearing a great number of sons. The spirits of fathers are bled dry by procreating a great number of sons.

The ornament of woman's body is jewelry. The ornament of woman's spirit is chastity.

The ocean is agitation. The desert is tranquility.

Ignoble people are never happy unless they find someone to worship them.

People imprisoned behind bars are free in spirit. People free of restraining bars are imprisoned by the world.

Man may love a woman without desiring her, because man's goal is beauty. It is, however, difficult for woman to love a man without desiring him, since woman's goal is children.

It is futile for us to attempt to live in desolate lands, since these bleed us dry.

Blood is visible freedom. Freedom is blood concealed.

Worldly glory is fortune's gift. Eternal glory is blood's gift.

Blood is the creation of the body. Creation is the blood of the spirit.

Freedom is a fire, but one that brings to life the phoenix of the spirit.

According to the moth's law, a flame is freedom. Flame is the proper heading for freedom in the law of people distinguished by their longing.

Is beauty freedom or freedom beauty?

Man deems woman's body fair game. Woman deems man's spirit fair game.

We should not trust a person who is ashamed for people to see him weep.

We are fascinated by what we love and destroyed by what we believe.

The mission of each life is happiness. The life of each mission requires the sacrifice of happiness.

Wisdom is the poetry of the wise, and poetry is the wisdom of the poets.

The spirit is trusted, even when the intellect disputes its veracity. Emotion is mistrusted even when the intellect lends it credence.

A slave who yearns for freedom is nobler than a freeman who consents to bondage.

Legal systems are traps that rigidify justice prematurely and snares to assault justice in full measure.

Like the antidote theriaca, legal systems are useful only on rare occasions, whereas they have the potential to cause a lot of harm.

The body is our exterior, which we ought to conceal. The spirit is our interior, which we ought to display.

The world is a body and the desert its spirit.

The tree is a hero that only falls once.

Freedom is the creature's argument for the Creator's existence.

The worst form of enmity between two men is that occasioned by a woman, for it endures until the cause is eliminated.

Woman and man are opposites in spirit and body. They cleave together to generate a third, incompatible creature, for the child establishes their unity while banishing them both.

Woman gives herself to a beggar who has given his self to her, but refuses herself to a sultan who has given her a kingdom while denying his self to her.

The poet's mission is to conceal, the philosopher's mission to reveal.

For woman, damage to her body is a defect, but a man's defect is damage to his mind.

Homelands are like fathers whose love for their children is many times greater than that of children for their fathers.

When woman becomes our paradise, we lose the paradise of the spirit.

A son who has never left home cannot be relied on, whether this refers to his country or his family.

Emigrants are not the only ones who weep for separation from a homeland. Countries also weep for sons who have left home.

Woman discerns the pulsing love in the heart of the man who loves her. She also discerns the pulse of love in the heart of a man who loves another woman.

Man thinks with his intellect. Woman thinks with her heart. This is the secret of woman's superiority over man.

Exile is a homeland for a man who possesses a prophetic aphorism. For a man who has lost an aphorism, a homeland is exile.

If people approach you wishing to serve you, know that you must possess wealth, power, or a secret.

Woman surrenders herself to a man who says he loves her, even when she knows he does not. Woman rejects a man who does not say he loves her, even if she knows he does.

Woman thinks even her Creator her declared enemy if He steals her companion from her.

Water is liquid time. Time is evanescent water.

Solitude aids us against the self. Company aids the self against us.

Defeat makes us alert, and victory leaves us lethargic.

What enters the mouth may poison the body. What emerges from the mouth may poison the spirit.

Imprisonment with a clear conscience is freedom, but freedom with a guilty conscience is imprisonment.

Crime is a sin against the rights of people. Sin is a crime against the rights of the Creator.

Loss of worldly pleasure is the price for perceiving the true nature of the world.

It is woman's destiny to give her heart to men whose spiritual depth she appreciates, but she does not object to giving her body to utter fools, provided they amuse her.

The fatherland is like a father who treats most roughly the child he loves.

Woman has no choice but to strip bare her body, since her spirit is a lost goal.

A wanton woman bares her body. A wanton man bares his spirit.

Man's spirit sheathes his body. Woman's body sheathes her spirit.

Sweat is the body's blood. Blood is the spirit's sweat.

The desert is not a land wasted by deprivation. The desert is a land that use has destroyed.

No nation's offspring are superior to those of another, since each person who thirsts for his truth is a hero and each who betrays his mission a knave.

There are two forms of insanity: that of a deranged person who is so overwhelmed by the world that he denies the spirit and that of a deranged person who is so overwhelmed by the spirit that he denies the world.

We need to renounce the world until we retain only the spirit's contemplation and the body's respiration.

When a man is inspired to feel contempt for his life by another person, that is abasement, but when he is inspired by an ideal it is heroism. Slaughtering our selves in the world is suicide. Slaughtering the world in our selves is sacrifice.

When a woman loves a man of property, she avenges herself on the property out of jealousy for its sway over its master. When a woman hates a man of property she avenges herself on his property out of hatred for its owner.

A wealthy person considers his wealth a lord. Whoever possesses a woman sees this woman as a lord. Anyone possessing a child considers the child a lord. Anyone possessing no wealth, no woman, and no child, sees the lord of lords as a lord.

The man who loses his battle with solitude finds no refuge save in a woman's embrace.

The ascetic is dead in life and alive in death.

Most living people are actually dead of worldliness. A minority of the deceased live on.

When wealthy, we are enslaved by women. When impoverished, we are enslaved by men.

Our existence in the desert is delimited. The existence of the desert in us is limitless.

The proof for death is life. The proof for life is death.

The desert, like deliverance, is an unknown beyond our powers of discovery.

The desert is divinity made manifest. Divinity is a hidden desert.

The desert is prophecy expressed physically. Prophecy is a desert camouflaged.

We lose the sons we marry to the daughters of strangers and gain the sons of strangers when we marry our daughters to them.

The time we kill kills us.

Time is that unknown entity that we always kill by talking but that always kills us by its deeds.

When I search for reality in the world I kill the world and my self. When I search for reality in my self, I bring to life the world and my self.

In the world, we are felons. In eternity, we are judges.

The desert is a homeland that has migrated.

Time is a vessel with life on its outside and annihilation inside.

If reality is a substance, then freedom is its essence. If reality is an essence, then freedom is its substance.

Beauty is the nobility of the body. Nobility is the beauty of the spirit.

Poverty that reforms us is nobler than riches that corrupt us.

Poverty that reforms us enriches us. Wealth that corrupts us impoverishes us.

The god we love we do not fear. The god we fear we do not love.

Freedom is the desert's water, and water is the body's freedom.

Language use exhausts the spirit just as the appetites exhaust the body.

If we cannot discover something to do with our time, time discovers something to do with us.

Man does not find time to spend money, since he is so preoccupied with making it. Woman does not find time to make money, since she is so preoccupied with spending it.

A tomb in the desert is everlasting sleep in a paradise of nonexistence.

Woman hears us, even if she is not paying attention, when we praise her. Woman does not hear us, even if she is paying attention, when we offer her counsel.

Water is blood that has lost its true color.

Wealth we give away is wealth that serves us. Wealth we retain is wealth we serve.

Anyone who fights in defense of a sanctuary is victorious even in defeat. Anyone who fights in defense of an idol is defeated even in victory.

The virtue of wealth is that it frees us from our need for wealth. The vice of wealth is that it cannot free us from death.

It is our hopes that slay us, not our derring-do.

Through memory the dead live. Through forgetfulness, the living die.

The creator vanishes with the death of his creation. The creation becomes eternal through the creator's death.

The desert has existed and will continue to exist. There was a time when we did not exist; eventually we will cease to exist.

We should hide our misery and our happiness. We hide our misery for fear our enemies will gloat. We conceal our happiness for fear our friends will gloat.

Glossary of Tuareg Terms

Amahagh and **Amazegh**: The singular forms, respectively, of Imuhagh and Imazeghen, which are names the Tuareg use for themselves. Both words mean dispossessed, plundered, lost, and noble.

Amnay: Seer, priest, diviner, and divine creature.

Anubi (Anubis): Son of an unknown father.

Anubis: In ancient Egypt, Anubis was the illegitimate son of Osiris, who accidentally cohabited with Nephthys, the wife of his brother Seth. She gave birth to Anubis, who became the god who attended the dead in the netherworld.

Ara: A word of contrasting meanings in Tuareg: either son or grandfather, offspring or progenitor.

Asaho: The constellation Canis Major or the star Sirius in it. Also known as Sau.

Azzka: In the ancient language, a tomb or dwelling, now used for a city.

Ba: The father, spirit, the nonexistent.

Hur: 'Guardian' in Tuareg, equivalent to the ancient Egyptian Horus.

Imazeghen: *See* Amahagh.

Imsikni: Marker, statue, or road sign.

Imuhagh: *See* Amahagh.

Iyghf: Head or intellect.

Iyla: The master, the existent, God.

Ma: The mother, mouth, cavity, water, natural characteristics, nature.

Ragh: The flaming, the yellow, the golden, the sun, the lord.

Sau: *See* Asaho.

Tin Hinan: Legendary matriarch of the Tuareg, a queen and priestess.

Wa: A child, birth, the existent.

Modern Arabic Literature

The American University in Cairo Press is the world's leading publisher of Arabic literature in translation.

For a full list of available titles, please go to:

mal.aucpress.com